VAL McCALL, ACE REPORTER?

At 6:00 A.M., the McCalls' phone began ringing off the hook.

After the first five or six calls, Val's stepfather came storming into her room. "Do you know what you've done?" he shouted, waking up Val.

"What's the matter?" Val muttered sleepily.

"Take a look at this!" Her stepfather stuck a copy of the *Angel Corners Gazette* in front of Val's face, but his hand was shaking so badly, she couldn't make out the print. Val grabbed the paper and began reading. Her stepfather had folded the paper open to her own column, "The Fifth-Grade Insider."

Welcome to Angel Corners! And beware! Every merchant on Main Street has doubled their prices for the Angel Corners Tourist Weekend. They are out to *zap* you!

"This is horrible!" Val threw back her covers and got out of bed. "I didn't write a word of this." Pacing the room, she read the rest of the column.

"This is crazy. Who did this?" she asked incredulously.

"That's what I'd like to know." Mr. McCall glared at her, his face flushing red.

ANGEL CORNERS

Val McCall, Ace Reporter?

BY **FRAN MANUSHKIN**

PUFFIN BOOKS

PUFFIN BOOKS
Published by the Penguin Group
Penguin Books USA Inc., 375 Hudson Street, New York, New York 10014, U.S.A.
Penguin Books Ltd, 27 Wrights Lane, London W8 5TZ, England
Penguin Books Australia Ltd, Ringwood, Victoria, Australia
Penguin Books Canada Ltd, 10 Alcorn Avenue, Toronto, Ontario, Canada M4V 3B2
Penguin Books (N.Z.) Ltd, 182-190 Wairau Road, Auckland 10, New Zealand

Penguin Books Ltd, Registered Offices: Harmondsworth, Middlesex, England

First published in the United States of America by Puffin Books,
a division of Penguin Books USA Inc., 1995
Published by arrangement with Chardiet Unlimited, Inc.

1 3 5 7 9 10 8 6 4 2

Copyright © Bernice Chardiet and Fran Manushkin, 1995
All rights reserved
Library of Congress Cataloging-in-Publication Data
Manushkin, Fran.
Val McCall, ace reporter? / Fran Manushkin.
p.   cm.—(Angel Corners; #4)
Summary: After a libelous story with her byline mysteriously appears in her
stepfather's newspaper, fifth grader Val McCall turns to her own guardian
angel and her friends in the Angel Club to help find who is responsible before
an innocent person is arrested.
ISBN 0-14-037201-6
[1. Guardian angels—Fiction. 2. Angels—Fiction. 3. Mystery and detective
stories.] I. Title. II. Series: Manushkin, Fran. Angel Corners; #4.
PZ7.M3195Val 1995 [Fic]—dc20 95-16162 CIP AC

Printed in the United States of America

For Barbara Seuling, who led me to the angels

CONTENTS

1

Val McCall's Perfect Life

Almost all the girls in Angel Corners envied Valentine McCall. Besides being the prettiest girl in the fifth grade, Val was also one of the nicest.

Her best friend, Lulu Bliss, sometimes teased Val, saying that she had a perfect life. "You live like a princess in a storybook. Just look at your house: it's so big and it's high up on a hill like a castle, *plus* you have closets full of gorgeous clothes, *and* you get along with your parents. You even get along with your stepsister. It's incredible."

This kind of talk made Val nervous. "Stop," she would beg. "You'll jinx me. Besides, my life isn't totally perfect. Zeb Burgess doesn't know I exist, remember?"

How could Lulu forget? Val was so gaga over Zeb, she couldn't utter a word around him. Her stunning red hair and violet eyes didn't help her feel the least bit confident with Zeb.

"I have a solution," Lulu told Val one day in Lulu's dad's video store. "Remember the videotape I shot of Zeb crossing the street last month? Why don't you play it over and over and practice talking to him. Then when you see him in person, you'll know what to say."

Val, who needed all the help she could get when it came to Zeb, had tried it. Night after night, she had sat leaning on plumped up pillows in her lacy canopy bed, watching the same footage of Zeb walking down Main Street. She had memorized every wave in his curly black hair, and she knew he had fourteen freckles. (She had used the pause button to stop the tape so she could count them.) And as Val watched Zeb, she chattered on and on. It was easy to talk to him when he was on the television.

After a few weeks of practice, Lulu told Val, "Okay, I think you're ready to try a conversation in person."

"I agree," said Val confidently. "I'll talk to Zeb the next time I have a chance. Today might be the day. Who knows?" As Val walked to her stepfather's office on that fateful Friday afternoon, she kept repeating phrases she'd memorized to say to Zeb.

Val McCall, Ace Reporter?

"Hello, Zeb. You probably don't know who I am, but I've had my eye on you . . ."

"Zeb Burgess! I've been meaning to talk to you!"

"Hi, Zeb. I'm Val. I'm in Ms. Fisher's class."

"Hey, Zeb, I wondered if you'd like to go to a movie with me sometime. . . ."

"Zeb, I dream of you every night. . . ."

They all sounded dreadful to her. But at least she was looking good in a ruffled white shirt and corduroy vest, jodhpurs, and granny boots.

Zeb wasn't all that Val had on her mind, however. She was on her way to put the finishing touches on her weekly newspaper column, "The Fifth-Grade Insider." Her stepfather owned the *Angel Corners Gazette* and had agreed to give her space, so long as she wrote professional, lively columns about town life. Val had written about the restoration of the Angel Clock—which had brought her together with her best friends, Lulu, Toby, and Rachel, to form the Angel Club—and then about the restoration of the train station.

She had interviewed Mayor Witty about his plans to turn Angel Corners into a national tourist site, the perfect New England town. She had even used her column to help gain acceptance for Sheriff Perkins's First-Offenders' Program. It gave first-time petty lawbreakers a chance to work at community service instead of paying fines or going to jail.

This week's article was all about the wonderful shopkeepers of Angel Corners. The paper was going to be sent throughout the state to attract folks to Angel Corners's first Tourist Weekend. Val's article was going to introduce the shop owners and the special qualities they each brought to their work.

She had so polished the article that there wasn't much left to do. It would take ten minutes to proofread and then—*zap*—she could send it to the printer by the touch of a key on her computer keyboard.

Val hurried along Main Street, thinking alternately about Zeb and her article. She was in such a good mood that she even waved hello to Felicia McWithers, who was back in town after being kicked out of boarding school. Felicia tossed her blond ponytail and pranced by without a word. Felicia's snobbery was as dependable as the sunrise over Angel Falls every morning.

Val took the *Gazette* office building steps two at a time. Her stepfather was the only one there, sitting in his corner office, talking on the phone. He gave a grin and a nod to his industrious stepdaughter as she sat down at one of the reporters' computers and spread out her notes.

When Mr. McCall hung up the phone, he called out to her, "Remember, Val, thousands of people will be reading the *Gazette* for the first time tomorrow—people from all over the state—so make it a good column!"

"It is!" she yelled back, reading out the first lines. "Calling all tourists!

"When you visit Angel Corners next weekend, don't miss Harry Bliss's Starlight Video store for the latest videos, popcorn, and all the movie trivia you could want from Harry and his daughter, Lulu.

"Antonio's Bakery can't be beat with their new line of scrumptious and healthy cookies and cakes, inspired by young Toby Antonio, baker, basketball star, and ballerina, with a healthy appetite.

"If your pet gets carsick on the way over, visit Dr. Summers's veterinary office. Both she and her daughter, Rachel, have a magic touch with animals."

"That's all well and good, dear," shouted Mr. McCall playfully, "but unless you want to be accused of a conflict of interest, you'd better report on all the businesses *not* owned by your friends' families, too."

"Oh, I cover them all! Derek Weatherby's Celestial Bookstore, Frank's Fabulous Clothing Store, Mom's travel agency, the café at the railroad station, even McWithers Stables—though they only let kids ride old nags."

Her list of establishments was cut short when Mr. McCall stood up from his chair to greet someone who had walked in behind Val.

"Well, Mr. Burgess," Mr. McCall said, striding out of his office, "glad you could make it. Come on in."

Val turned, expecting to see Zeb's father there to place an ad or something. Instead, she got an eyeful of Zeb himself, now following her father back to his office. Val opened her mouth to say "hi," but nothing came out. Zeb hadn't noticed anyway. He just looked at the floor, a little embarrassed, as he walked by.

Zeb closed the office door behind him, and Val was torn between finishing her column and sneaking up to the keyhole to listen. Sense got the better of her, though it was a difficult struggle, and she put the final touches on her column.

Suddenly the door to the office opened, and Val heard her father speak. "Thanks for coming, Zeb. The *Gazette* is growing so fast, we need more delivery boys than ever. But I'm giving you the hilliest part of town, near Angel Falls. Are you up to it?"

"Sure, Mr. McCall. Thanks. I've got my mountain bike. Hills are no trouble at all, sir."

"Fine, fine," said the newspaper publisher. "You can finish filling out these forms in the employees' lounge and start work in the morning. Here." Val's father fumbled in his pocket for change. "Have a soda on me while you're at it."

"Thanks an awful lot, Mr. McCall. I'll be here

bright and early tomorrow morning for my route. I promise."

Zeb was being awfully grateful for a delivery job, thought Val. Before he finished shaking hands with her father, however, Val was up and on her way to the bathroom. She couldn't bear to face him, even after all Lulu's coaching.

She gazed out the bathroom door as Zeb made his way to the employees' lounge, bought himself a soda, and sat down to finish his paperwork.

"Come on," she urged herself, "get over there and talk to him!" But Zeb's blue shirt stopped her. It matched the color of his eyes. She took one step and chickened out.

She ran back into the bathroom and combed and recombed her hair. Finally, she was ready to go. One deep breath . . . but she panicked. *I can't do it.* She heard Zeb push his chair back and crack his knuckles. She waited an extra long time until she was sure he was gone. Then she carefully opened the door just in time to see Zeb leaving.

Val went over to Zeb's chair and sat down in it. She consoled herself. *Zeb will be here a lot now that he's working for Dad. I'll have other chances to talk to him.*

"Did you finish your column?" asked Val's stepdad, waking her from her Zeb daydream.

"Oh, yes," she answered. "It's going to be a very special column."

"Give it a read-over before you send it to the printer," Mr. McCall reminded her. "Remember, when your name is at the top of a column, you are responsible for it. Proofread it carefully."

"I know." Val nodded her head solemnly.

"And remember, your deadline is five o'clock sharp," said Mr. McCall. "I'll be in my office if you need me."

But Val fell back to daydreaming, and visions of wedding announcements soon filled her head.

"Valentine McCall, Reporter, Weds Zeb Burgess, Business Executive . . . " No, that wasn't right. "Valentine McCall, Reporter, Weds Zeb Burgess, Country's Youngest Millionaire." That was more like it. She knew she was being silly, but she couldn't help it.

Suddenly the front door of the office closed sharply, waking her fully. She looked up at the clock and realized she had only five minutes to get her story to the printer.

She ran to her computer station, called up her article, and zapped it to the printer—without rereading it. Then she ran home to call Lulu and tell her all about Zeb's new job at the newspaper.

And that was the first step in the total collapse of Valentine McCall's perfect life.

2

Extra! Extra!

The next morning at 6:00 A.M., just after Zeb finished his first deliveries, the McCalls' phone
began ringing off the hook.

After the first five or six calls, Val's stepfather
came storming into her room. "Do you know what
you've done?" he shouted, waking up Val.

"What's the matter?" Val muttered sleepily.

"Take a look at this!" Her stepfather stuck a copy
of the *Angel Corners Gazette* in front of Val's face.

She tried to focus on the paper, but her stepdad's
hand was trembling so badly, she couldn't make out
the print. Val grabbed the paper and began reading.
Her stepfather had folded the paper open to "The
Fifth-Grade Insider."

"Welcome to Angel Corners!" Val's column began. "And beware! Every merchant on Main Street has doubled their prices for the weekend! They are out to *zap* you!"

Val gulped. "I don't understand. I didn't write this."

"Keep reading," said her stepfather grimly.

"Watch out for Antonio's Bakery," Val read on. "They claim to have low-calorie treats, but it's well known that Mr. Antonio puts lard in his piecrusts.

"And as for our railroad station restoration: ask Mayor Witty how much money he put into his own pockets from that project."

"This is horrible!" Val threw back her covers and got out of bed. "I didn't write a word of this." Pacing the room, Val read the rest of the column. Instead of celebrating Angel Corners, it managed to insult almost every business in town. "If your pet is sick, stay away from Dr. Deborah Summers!" The column screamed. "She's poison to pussycats!

"This is crazy. Who did this?" Val asked incredulously.

"That's what I'd like to know." Mr. McCall glared at her, his face flushing red. "Did you proofread the column before you sent it to the printer?"

"Of course I did!" she answered back, and then gulped and turned pale. "Uh-oh." She remembered how she had fled to the bathroom and then spent her time in the lounge daydreaming about Zeb, until she almost missed her deadline. Val swallowed hard.

"I didn't," she said very softly.

Mr. McCall groaned as the phone rang again. "I'll take care of you later, young lady." After he stormed out of the room, Val tossed on her bathrobe and followed him downstairs.

"What's going on?" Val's stepsister, Tracy, asked, still rubbing sleep from her eyes. She was six years old and stood on the stairs in her Little Mermaid pajamas.

"Read it and weep." Val tossed her the paper.

Tracy burst into tears. "You *know* I can't read, yet."

"I'm sorry," Val said, scooping Tracy up in her arms for comfort. "Come downstairs and I'll explain it."

Val found her mother sitting in the breakfast nook, a red kimono pulled tightly around her. She seemed to be shivering as she gazed at the *Gazette*. She hadn't touched her coffee.

"Mom, I'm so sorry," Val began. "This is some sick person's idea of a joke."

"Some joke." Mrs. McCall read from the paper: "Rumor has it that Hortense Heft and her bridegroom are splitsville."

"But they just got married." Tracy's big blue eyes grew wide.

"None of this is true," Val explained. "Somebody got hold of my column and rewrote it. They said terrible things about lots of people."

"Uh-oh." Tracy giggled.

"It's not funny!" Mrs. McCall said. "Every person in this column is entitled to sue us. It will be the end of the *Gazette.*"

"But they can't," Val said. "It's all made-up."

"Val." Her mother made a weak attempt at a smile. "Everything in this article can be read as libel—published lies. People sue over libel all the time. And since your stepfather and I own the newspaper, that means we are the ones who are going to get sued!"

"Gosh," said Tracy.

"Gosh, indeed," responded Mrs. McCall, and waited for her other daughter to say something.

Val didn't know what to say. She burst into tears. "But, I didn't write it! Someone must have got—gotten to it before I sent it in and be—because I didn't read it over . . . I didn't see it! I'm so sorry, Mom." She burst into fresh tears for a minute and then raised her head. There was an angry look in her eyes. "I've got to find out who did this! I've got to find them and make them apologize to everyone in Angel Corners!"

"Val," Mrs. McCall said calmly, "the first thing to do is to remedy the situation the best we can. Your stepfather is taking all the phone calls—and you can imagine they aren't pleasant—and apologizing on behalf of the *Gazette*. I am going to write an apology to be mailed to all the subscribers, not to mention the thousands of people statewide who received this special tourist edition."

"What can I do?" asked Val.

"We'd like you to write an apology to be printed in the next issue of the paper. After that, we'll talk about who did it. And we'll discuss the responsibility of having a newspaper column under your own name. . . . Do you understand?"

"Yes, Mom," said Val sadly. "Why didn't I pay attention to my job? Then none of this would have happened!"

Val had never seen her mother so worried. She trudged back upstairs and got dressed. It was definitely a jeans and sweatshirt day. There was a fog rising from Angel Stream, and everything looked gray and damp. Val looked at the clock—6:30 A.M. She heard the phone ring again. *What can I do?* she wondered. *I have to find out who did this to me. And what will happen when Lulu and Toby and Rachel read my column? They'll never speak to me again!*

"Mom," called Val as she raced down the stairs, "can I go over to Lulu's to apologize in person?

She'll never talk to me again—and neither will Toby or Rachel—unless I get to them first. Please? Maybe they can help me find out who did this."

"All right, dear," said Val's mother with a sigh, "but I want you to start working on your apology as soon as you get home."

"Can I come, too?" asked Tracy eagerly.

"No, little pumpkin," said Val, giving her stepsister a kiss. "I have to do this by myself." Val zipped up her windbreaker and walked out the backdoor. The fog enveloped her and she remembered that she hadn't eaten anything. *Well, what's food when the whole town is turned against you?* she thought dramatically.

Soon Val was standing at the door of Lulu Bliss's apartment, above Starlight Video. She rang the bell. Nobody answered, so she rang it again.

In a few minutes, Mr. Bliss appeared at the door, his black hair rumpled with sleep. He yawned. "Val, what's wrong?"

"Uh . . . something important . . . You're not going to like it. Can I wake up Lulu and tell both of you together?"

"Sure." Mr. Bliss nodded, and Val walked past him to Lulu's room.

The sleeves of a red sweater drooped out of Lulu's dresser, and Tom Hanks smiled down from her new poster of Forrest Gump.

"Get up," Val urged Lulu, giving her a little shake. Lulu's head sprang from her pillow like a jack-in-the-box.

"Wha—what's wrong?" Lulu blinked quickly, surprised by the bright bedroom light her dad had turned on. She instinctively looked at her clock. "Val! It's not even 7:00!"

Val sat down on the side of the bed and took a deep breath. "Lulu," she began in a shaky voice, "Mr. Bliss, this is absolutely terrible news. . . ."

"What is it?" Lulu demanded. She was awake now.

"Um . . . someone rewrote my column in the *Gazette*. And—and . . . they said terrible things about some people in town . . . and your dad was one of them."

"What do you mean?" Mr. Bliss and Lulu both looked alarmed.

"Here." Val handed Mr. Bliss the paper, and he began reading aloud: "Be sure to avoid Starlight Video at all costs! Mr. Bliss is friendly, all right, but he will *zap* you with the tapes he rents and sells! They are pirated! They come from China, where they are made with child labor! That's how his prices can be so cheap."

Mr. Bliss turned a nasty shade of pink.

Lulu leaped out of bed, almost tripping over a stack of movie magazines. "Let me see that!" After a quick glance, Lulu glared at her best friend. "How did this happen? This is terrible!"

"I know, and I'm going to fix it, I promise." Val looked back at her friend pleadingly. "I would never do something like this to you, Lulu. Someone rewrote my article before it got printed. I had to come here and explain, so you would understand. But, I'll find out who did this! I promise!" There was a touch of panic in her voice.

"This could put me out of business!" Mr. Bliss shouted. "And wait until the government sees this! They'll think I've broken every law in the book."

Val blurted out another apology. "Mr. Bliss, everyone in town knows how nice you are and that you wouldn't do this."

"How about people from out of town?" Mr. Bliss asked. "This is going all over the state, remember?"

Val's eyes filled with tears. "I'm so sorry . . . I'm so sorry. . . ."

Lulu didn't know who to feel more sorry for—her dad or her best friend. "We're going to find out who did this, Val, and we're going to start right now!"

Mr. Bliss stalked out of the bedroom mumbling, "Sue the *Gazette!*"

"I'll get dressed." Lulu took off her pajamas and put on her Cozumel Island sweatshirt and jeans. She was still tanned from the snorkeling vacation she and her dad had just taken.

"Lulu," Val begged, "I have to go tell Toby and Rachel's parents. Please come with me, okay? I feel so awful."

"Of course I will," said Lulu faithfully.

As they left, they saw Lulu's dad pacing the living-room floor, on the portable phone to his new girlfriend, who was also his accountant. "Sally?" he was saying. "I'm sorry to wake you, but I need your business advice. Something horrible has happened. . . ."

"Dad talks to Sally a lot," Lulu said with a sigh. "But I'm getting used to it." Then she shivered. "Whew! This fog is so intense, it reminds me of something out of a movie."

"Everything reminds you of a movie," Val said, trying to interject some humor.

After their long walk through the fog, Rachel's lit-up house was a welcome sight. "Animals wake up really early," Lulu said, "so the people who live with them must, too."

Rachel and Dr. Summers were in the kitchen wearing white smocks and bottle-feeding two lambs. "Hi!" Rachel greeted them. "These lambs were born prematurely, so Mom and I are their moms for a while. Hey," she said, glancing up at the clock, "Lulu, you never get up this early. Is something wrong?"

"Yes. Very wrong," Lulu said, putting her arm

around Val. "Go ahead and tell them," she whispered.

"Um," Val gulped. "This doesn't get easier . . ."

"What's the matter?" Rachel brushed her blond bangs out of her eyes. "Tell me, Val. It'll be okay."

"Um . . . this news is for both of you." Val told Dr. Summers. She opened the *Gazette* and tried to read it out loud. "I can't! I just can't."

"Here." Lulu handed the paper to Rachel's mother. "You'd better sit down while you read this."

"I'll hold that lamb," Val said quickly. She hugged the animal close, hiding her face in its soft fleece.

As Dr. Summers read the column, all the blood seemed to drain from her face. "Oh no!"

"What is it?" Rachel rushed over to see. "Oh my gosh!" she burst out. "This is horrible!" Her shout startled the lamb she was feeding, and he began bleating. Val's lamb joined in.

"How did this happen?" Dr. Summers shouted over the din.

"I . . . uh . . . didn't read over my column before I sent it to the printer," admitted Val.

"This issue must not be delivered." Dr. Summers's voice was firm.

"It's too late." Val looked at her helplessly. "It's already been delivered to towns all around us."

"It can't be!" Dr. Summers shouted. "This is

going to ruin my practice." She grabbed both lambs from the girls and went through the adjoining door to her office to put them back in their cages. "Val, I'm calling your father at once. This is his responsibility."

"No, it's mine," Val said. "And I'm going to try and find the culprit."

"You mean *we're* going to find the culprit," Rachel spoke up. Her heart-shaped face was set in a stubborn expression. Rachel was a quiet girl, but loyal to the core.

She unbuttoned her white smock and reached behind the kitchen door for her jacket. "I'll come with you and Lulu right now."

"We have to go to Toby's house," said Val. "The Antonios haven't heard the news yet."

"Mom, I'm going to help Val and Lulu," Rachel called.

Her mother was already on the phone, and she waved Rachel off. "Just be back by the afternoon," she yelled.

"Wow!" said Rachel when they walked out into the fog. "What is it with this weather?"

"It's just about how I feel," reflected Val, "foggy and miserable."

"Come on," said Lulu, "let's hold hands so it doesn't seem so bad."

Soon they saw a little golden island of light

emerging from the fog. It was the glow of Antonio's Bakery.

"Of course, all the Antonios are up," Rachel said. "Bakers get up earlier than veterinarians. Some even bake all night long."

The heavenly scent of fresh bread greeted the girls as they walked inside. Val inhaled deeply, momentarily cheered by the warmth and sweetness in the air.

Mr. Antonio greeted them. "Good morning!" he said cheerfully. "Foggy days are great for my business. Everyone wants a cozy breakfast with fresh rolls and muffins. It never fails."

Val stood, shuffling nervously from one foot to the other.

Lulu put her arm around her. "Shall I tell them?" she whispered.

"No," Val answered, "I have to do it. . . . Um . . . Mr. Antonio, you'd better put down that whipped-cream cake before I show you this."

"What's the matter?" Toby came in, stirring some batter. She was wearing a white apron and her long braid was coiled up under a net. "Val, you look awful."

"That's because I *did* something awful," Val said. "I mean it wasn't as awful as the person who wrote this . . ." She handed the *Gazette* to Mrs. Antonio, who began to read it.

"Oh my goodness," Toby's mother gasped, and sat down.

Toby's father read over his wife's shoulder and soon started shaking. "Young lady, do you know what you've done?" He pointed his finger at Val. "It's taken this family twenty-five years to build up this business. And you're about to destroy it in one day."

Toby took the paper from her mother.

"I didn't write it!" Val protested. "You've got to believe me! But I'm going to find the person who did, and when I do . . ." Val's voice died away.

"You'd better find them *pronto!*" Toby glared at her. Val had never seen Toby so angry, and she'd known her ever since they were two year olds.

"I'll find out who did it . . . at least, I'm going to try," Val promised. "Can we go upstairs to your room and talk about it? I'll explain the whole thing."

Toby nodded. "Let's go."

"Since we are all here," said Rachel, "we'll make this a meeting of the Angel Club. Finding the culprit is obviously our next project."

"Right," Lulu agreed. "Maybe, together, we can fix this mess."

As Toby, Rachel, Lulu, and Val hurried upstairs, another angel club was about to meet farther up.

3

Clouds of Confusion

F lorinda, the Queen of the Angels, was ringing a huge celestial bell and calling, "All angels-in-training! Please report at once to the center of the Clouds of Confusion. And, I mean at once!"

A great flutter of wings filled the sky, as angels ascended and descended from all directions. It certainly was difficult, even for angels, to find the center of the Clouds of Confusion, because the clouds swirled and shifted direction every few seconds.

"I'm here!" called Merribel, who had wild red hair and rumpled wings. Merrie managed to find her way through the clouds first, because she was one angel who was almost always in a state of confusion.

Celeste came fluttering in, with Serena behind her. "Ha! I told you Merrie would find her way through the clouds first!"

There was so much confusion that a number of lesser angels snuck in, hiding behind the shifting clouds. One, called Emerald, who was quite young and impatient, for an angel, hid directly above Merrie's halo so she could get a good view of Florinda. Emerald had green pigtails, with a gold flute tucked into one of them. Her short purple dress and slippers were almost as scruffy as Lulu's jeans and sneakers.

Florinda gazed around the clouds that filled the endless sky. "Where is Amber?" she asked. "I especially want Amber to be here."

"Oh, I passed her light years away," bragged Merrie. "She must have gotten lost—and she says *I* have *my* head in the clouds!"

"I'm here." Amber's sensible voice pierced through the clouds, almost uncovering Emerald's hiding place. "I was not lost. I was taking time to compose myself."

"Why is that, dear?" asked Florinda.

"Well, every time you call us all in a rush like that, it means that one of us is going to earth—to

Angel Corners. Merrie went to help Rachel; Serena went to help Toby; Celeste went to help Lulu; and there is only one member of the Angel Club left without her guardian angel: Val. I was thinking you wanted me to go down to earth and help her, so I was composing myself."

Florinda smiled broadly at her most serious and well-poised angel-in-training. "So, you think I mean to send you down to help Valentine McCall?"

Amber looked at her hands in her lap. "Yes, I think so," she said with embarrassment.

"What kind of problems do you think someone like Val would have?" asked Florinda. "She has a loving, open family, friends, a good head for school, and a good heart. . . ."

"Well, sometimes, just because you seem to live a perfect life doesn't mean that only perfect things happen to you—at least not on earth. And, I was watching Val yesterday when she made a terrible mistake. So, I've been waiting for your summons. You are sending me, aren't you?"

"Yes, Amber, I am," said Florinda.

"All right!" cried out Serena, and the four angels-in-training slapped their hands together in a high five, like they'd seen the Angel Club do.

"Calm down, angels," called Florinda. "I am impressed, Amber, that you were paying such close attention to what was happening yesterday while the rest of us were busy with our centennial Stars and Rainbows Dance. Does anyone else know what Amber knows?"

The other angels-in-training shook their heads solemnly, and suddenly from near Merrie came a tickling run of flute notes. Emerald poked her head out from behind a shifting cloud.

"I know, Florinda!" she called. "I saw what happened!"

"Emerald, dear," chided Florinda, "you are not supposed to be here."

At that, Emerald shrank behind her cloud and played a sort of apologetic tune on her flute.

"Okay, you may stay—but just this once. You haven't even earned your halo, yet, and these are my most advanced students. But, please, keep quiet and sit still."

"Amber, would you fill in your fellow angels?" asked Florinda.

Amber rose. "Val was supposed to file her column for the *Angel Corners Gazette* last night, but she was daydreaming so much about Zeb Burgess that she almost missed her deadline. And while Val was daydreaming, someone snuck in and rewrote her article to say awful things about all the good people of Angel Corners. When the paper hit people's doorsteps this morning, everyone blew up! And Val is in big trouble."

"Did you see who rewrote the column, Amber?" asked Florinda gently.

"No," answered Amber. "I confess, I was day-dreaming about Zeb and Val, too."

"Let this be a lesson to all of you that you can't guard your children by falling into the same traps they do! They are human, while we are angels! We probably couldn't have prevented such a thing from happening. . . . But, let this be a lesson for us *all*, myself included."

Florinda bowed her head as the angels exchanged glances. They had never seen Florinda admit to any imperfection before—and yet, she was always saying she didn't expect them to be perfect. The angels had a lot to think about.

"Florinda," said Amber cautiously, "do you really want *me* to go and fix this mess?"

"I'm counting on you, Amber. Not to fix this mess, but to help guide your child, Val, through it. She needs her guardian angel now more than ever, don't you think?"

"Yes, Florinda," said Amber.

Suddenly, a flute was heard again. "Can I go, too?" begged Emerald.

"Most certainly not," said Florinda sternly. "How could you even think of such a thing? But you may come forward and join in the blessing when we send Amber down to earth." Florinda focused on

Amber again. "Why, Amber, you are trembling. Come here and tell me what's wrong."

"Well," Amber began in a shaky voice, "it's been so easy to be confident here, surrounded by all the other angels . . . but to actually face my girl . . . on earth . . . by myself . . ." Amber's voice faded away.

"That's a jewel of a different color," interjected Emerald.

Florinda hugged her amber-colored angel-in-training close to her. "You know that I don't expect you to be perfect"—the other angels-in-training all exchanged glances again—"I just expect you to be good-hearted and to try hard. I know you will do that."

"Now . . ." She resumed her classroom manner. "Let's review the rules for visiting earth."

"Rule one!" Emerald called out. "Only your girl can see you."

"Rule two!" Merrie said. "You can take any form you want. I was a bird."

"I pretended to be a train!" said Celeste. "I felt so powerful!"

"Rule three," Serena interrupted, "you can't appear in your angelic form unless your child asks for you."

Florinda turned to Amber. "Please recite the last rule."

"Remember that humans are sometimes surprised when they see an angel," said Amber, "so proceed with caution."

"I'll play you a good-bye song on my flute," Emerald volunteered. She plucked the tiny flute from behind her ear and tooted a friendly tune.

"That was nice of you. Thank you." Amber smiled.

"I wish I were going with you," said Emerald with a pout.

Then Amber set her steady eyes on Angel Corners, opened her smooth wings, and flew down to the top of the ginkgo tree in Val's backyard.

She made herself comfortable there, waiting for Val to summon her. Amber had a while to wait, for the Angel Club meeting was going on and on.

A few doughnut crumbs sat on otherwise-empty plates, and the Angel Club was sprawled over four armchairs, looking dazed.

"We've been going around in circles," Toby moaned, "and we still don't know what to do."

"I think we should review our list of suspects and then go talk to them," suggested Rachel. "We have to start somewhere. My mother's business is at stake!"

"So is my dad's video store!" said Lulu angrily.

"And my family's bakery," Toby said for the zillionth time.

"Look," said Val, "we've been through this. How many times can I apologize? Please, let's just get a plan going and stop fighting."

"Sorry, Val," murmured Lulu, reaching out to take her friend's hand.

Toby picked up the pad of paper on which the Angel Club had written the names of all the suspects they could think of.

"Chet Harris. Thanks to Lulu, he's still in jail for robbing Mrs. McCall's travel agency and Derek's bookstore—"

Lulu took an impromptu bow.

"Mr. McCall was in the office, but there's absolutely no motive, unless . . ."

Val interrupted. "Toby Antonio! Don't you dare suggest that Dad would sabotage his own newspaper, not to mention his reputation. If you had seen how upset he was this morning . . ." Val's eyes, already red-rimmed, teared up again.

"Of course he wouldn't," said Toby. "But he was there, so we had to mention him. But I think we can scratch him off the list."

"Well, for that matter," said Val, "you might as well consider me a suspect!"

"Okay, girls," said Rachel, standing up. "We're not getting anywhere. Toby, who else is on the list?"

"There's Zeb Burgess and Felicia McWithers."

"Zeb wouldn't do a thing like that!" said Val.

"How do you know, Val? You don't really know him, do you? You've never even talked to him!" countered Toby. Everyone's tempers were high, and Toby had no intention of holding back for fear of hurting her friend's feelings.

"Toby!" pleaded Val.

"Well?" said Toby.

"Okay, he was there."

"That leaves Felicia," said Rachel, looking out a window. "She certainly caused me enough trouble when I first moved here—stealing the Angel Club money from me and then Mayor Witty's puppy from Mom's clinic!"

"And I heard she got kicked out of that boarding school her parents sent her to," said Lulu.

"I did see her a few blocks away from the office as I went in to file my column," volunteered Val. "But, I never saw her in the office."

"I think we have to include her," said Toby, "just on the grounds that she is a mean troublemaker and has had it out for the Angel Club ever since we got together!"

"Okay," said Rachel, "let's split up. Toby and I will talk to Felicia, and Val and Lulu will talk to Zeb. Do you think you can do that, Val?"

"Of course I can!" snapped Val. "But right now,

I have to get home and start working on my apology for the next issue of the *Gazette.* "

"Meeting adjourned," declared Toby.

On the way out, Rachel took Val aside. "Maybe you should think about calling on your guardian angel. You sure could use her now."

The suggestion brought tears to Val's eyes again. *How could my life have fallen apart so fast?* she thought. "That's a good idea, Rachel. Thanks."

"Hey," called Lulu, "the Angel Club's first anniversary is coming up. Now would be the perfect time for your angel to come, so we would all know our angels when it comes time to have our party!"

"First things first, Lulu," said Val. "I don't feel much like thinking about parties right now."

The Angel Club members wandered outside and went their separate ways. In a minute, the stoop outside Toby's house was once again covered in fog, as if no one had ever been there.

As she walked through the gate into her own backyard, Val had a sudden enlightening thought. Her life *had* been pretty near perfect. Her parents loved her. She had every creature comfort. Now, for the first time in her life, she didn't know how to cope with a problem she was facing. And her parents couldn't make it all better, and all the creature

CORNERS

ANGEL

comforts in the world wouldn't make it go away. Her life was *not* perfect.

"Oh," she cried out, "Angel, if you are listening . . . would you come now? I need you very much."

"I am already here." The fog cleared, and Val saw—on the weather vane on top of her house—her shimmering, glittering angel.

32

4

Warm and Cozy,
Cold and Icy

"**A**mber, reporting for duty!" sang the exquisite angel. She saluted like a general. Then she opened her wings—unlike any general Val had ever seen!—and flew down, landing next to Val.

"Oh my!" Val was almost speechless. Then she cried out, "Oh, I need you so much!"

"That's why I came." Amber opened her arms and enclosed Val in her warm wings. How soft they felt, and how soothing. "Come," said her angel softly. "Let me take you back to your warm room."

Enveloped in Amber's wings, Val felt her feet leaving the ground. "Oh gosh!" she gasped.

Slowly and steadily, Amber and Val rose over the fence and the ginkgo tree. "Now I'll signal a right turn," Amber said, flashing a row of lights on her right wing. They tilted to the right and flew right through the open window of Val's room.

"I always follow the traffic rules," Amber explained. "There!" She beamed, setting Val down on her couch. "A perfect landing."

Val sat, speechless and a little dizzy.

"I'll light a fire," Amber suggested. Val nodded, still dazed. Amber waved her arm at the empty fireplace across from Val's canopied bed. Birch logs suddenly appeared, flared up into flame, and settled down to a soft, warm crackling.

Val's violet eyes stared in amazement. Had she just flown? She had! Was an angel actually in her bedroom? She was!

"I must get you out of these wet clothes. I don't want you to catch cold," Amber said in her sensible voice. She touched Val lightly, and her wet outfit was replaced by a pumpkin-colored robe and matching slippers.

"Thank you," Val said, pinching herself to be totally sure she was awake.

"Hot chocolate?" Amber offered, and a mug of frothy cocoa appeared on the nearby table.

"Oh, gosh, I don't know what to say." Val smiled. She was definitely alert now and feeling better than she had all day.

"Don't worry," Amber assured her. "I know

angels can be awesome. Sit back and sip your chocolate, and then you can tell me everything."

Val nodded. After some sips of cocoa and a long look at her angel, Val felt less awed and more ready to talk. "Amber! That's such a nice name." Val smiled. "Oh, Amber . . ." Her face grew pale, and her voice shook. "I have never felt so lost in my life."

"Your confidence has been shaken," said her angel. "Hasn't it?"

"Yes." Val nodded. "All the problems I've ever had before seem so small compared to this one. I don't know what to do . . ."

Amber gazed at her sympathetically. "It *is* scary! Why don't you tell me in your own words what has happened?"

"Amber, it's gotten so big, it's hard to know where to start!"

"It's best to start at the beginning and tell me everything," Amber said, soothingly. She sat down next to Val and put a comforting, strengthening arm around her shoulders.

"I was excited to put the last touches on my article and send it off to the printer. On the way, I remember I waved to Felicia—she's a snobby girl in my class who is always angry at the Angel Club—"

"Yes, we know about Felicia McWithers up at the Angel Academy. Poor dear. Go on," said Amber.

Poor dear? thought Val, but she was not about to question her angel.

"Well, I waved to Felicia before going into the office. I sat at the computer and was typing in my final changes when I heard Zeb Burgess walk in and my stepfather greet him. Zeb is . . ."

"Yes, dear, we know about Zeb, too."

"Okay," said Val, blushing a little. *How much did they know, these angels?* "They went into Dad's office and, well, I was tempted to eavesdrop, but I didn't. I swear I didn't."

"Please don't swear, Val. It's so unangelic."

"Yes, Amber," replied Val. "When Zeb came out of Dad's office, I couldn't face him, so I ran to the bathroom while he filled out his employment papers in the employees' lounge. I waited a long time. I thought I might go and try and talk to him, but I am such a coward . . ."

"Now, Val," said Amber gently, "you are hardly a coward! Who was it who marched to each of her best friends' houses this morning to break the news? Didn't that take courage? I think you are just scared to talk to Zeb, because he means a lot to you, and you are angelically innocent when it comes to boys."

"I *will* talk to Zeb," Val insisted. "I just wasn't ready before. And I *was* courageous to go to the Angel Club and try to explain what happened, only I don't *know* what happened."

"That's what we're here to find out," said Amber, getting Val back on track.

"So, I waited and waited. I heard him leave the lounge, but it took him forever to actually leave the newspaper office. I listened for the front door to close. Finally, I heard it and came out of hiding."

Val paused.

"This is a little embarrassing, but I want to tell you everything." Val took a deep breath. "I went and sat down on the chair that Zeb had been sitting in and I started daydreaming about us, about Zeb and me getting married." Val winced with embarrassment.

"Oh, dear," Amber clapped her hands. "What a lovely daydream. I am so glad you like this Zeb so much. It will help you when the time comes to talk to him. And that time may be coming sooner than you think."

"What do you mean?" asked Val.

"Is that the end of your story?" responded Amber, not answering Val's question.

"Well, almost. I sat there until Dad came in and warned me that it was almost deadline, and he asked if I had sent my article to the printer. And he asked whether I had proofread it."

"Then?" prodded Amber.

"Amber, I knew what I had written, and I knew I had typed it perfectly. It was so late, I just pushed the button to send it to the printer without looking at it again. I know I shouldn't have . . ."

"Enough remorse, my dear, it will only ruin your complexion at this point," Amber said. "Cheer up. We have work to do if we are going to solve this mystery. And you are going to have to be more courageous than you were even this morning. But you are braver than you think."

"Do you think so?" Val asked hopefully.

"Of course. And, remember, I'm here to help you." Amber smiled. "I'm great at solving all kinds of puzzles. I've always gotten high marks in Heavenly Logic."

Val smiled. "High marks! That's funny—I mean—considering where you come from. You know, heaven on high . . . high marks?"

"Yes, of course." Amber smiled, but her face quickly turned serious again.

Val took a big sip of chocolate. It had a minty taste, and new whipped cream appeared on the top as soon as she licked any off.

"Now," said Amber, "there are three points of your story that need some sleuthing. First, what was Zeb Burgess doing there?"

"He's going to deliver papers for the *Gazette*," said Val.

"Isn't he a bit old to begin delivering newspapers? He's ahead of you in class, isn't he?"

"Well, yes, but he's not old enough for real work."

"Hmmmm, still it seems a bit odd that at age thirteen he would start delivering papers. Don't boys of nine or ten do that sort of thing?" Amber persisted.

"I don't know!" said Val exasperatedly. "Maybe he needs the money!"

"Now, now, dear," Amber reassured her, stroking Val's hair, "it's just a question I am asking. No harm in that, is there?"

"No," mumbled Val into her hot chocolate, "I guess not."

"Second." Amber charged ahead. "Zeb took a long time leaving the newspaper office after filling out his forms. I wonder why. How long, would you say?"

"I don't know! I was standing in the bathroom! And I wasn't wearing a watch." Val's temper had a short fuse, as Amber was discovering.

"Hold on, now," said Amber. "I am just asking questions, remember?"

"Yes," Val sighed into her hot chocolate.

"Third, someone changed your article while you were either in the bathroom or in the employees' lounge."

"Amber," said Val with a choked voice, "if you're trying to get me to say that Zeb Burgess fudged my article on his way out, you're crazy. He wouldn't do that! He just wouldn't. I know he wouldn't." Val kept repeating herself until she realized that Amber was looking at her strangely.

"I didn't say he did do it," said the angel. "I'm just pointing out that someone did."

"Anyway," said Val, "I promised the Angel Club that I would go with Lulu to talk to him about it. And I will, too."

"Would you mind if I were there when you did, just to back you up?" asked Amber with her soft eyes gleaming.

"Oh, Amber," cried Val, "I didn't mean to get angry at you! I know you are here to help and, yes, I want you to be there, very much! I don't have the foggiest idea what I will say!"

"Good. Meanwhile, you have an apology to write, and I have some sleuthing to do around Angel Corners."

"Sleuthing?" asked Val.

"Just flying around to see if I can pick up any scuttlebutt," she answered. "I'll certainly let you know if I hear anything! And, remember, you just have to call me, and I'll be by your side."

"Thank you, Amber," said Val.

"You're very welcome," said Amber, and she was gone.

Val set down her mug of hot chocolate and

plopped down on her bed, trying to absorb all that had happened. Finally, she calmed down enough to pick up the phone. She pressed number one on her speed-dial to call Lulu.

"Guess what?" were Val's first words.

"Your angel came," Lulu said.

"How did you know?"

"You said you were going to call her, remember? What's her name? What does she look like? Can she help you?"

"Her name is Amber, and she has amber hair and an amber dress."

"She's color coordinated just like you," Lulu teased. "Really, Val, I'm so glad she's here. What did she say?"

"First I've got to tell you what she did," Val said breathlessly. "She wrapped me in her wings, and— we flew, Lulu."

"You're kidding!" Lulu nearly shouted. "Celeste never did that with me. I'm going to ask her why not the next time I see her."

"Oh, and she lit a fire in my fireplace with a wave of her hand, . . . and she made me a mug of hot chocolate with whipped cream that keeps refilling!" Val took a sip from the mug. The chocolate was still steaming hot and there was as much whipped cream as ever.

"Angels are awesome," Lulu said happily. "Val,

listen, I want to hear everything that Amber said and did, but I can't now. Sally Jillian is coming for supper tonight, and Dad and I are about to make an amaretto chocolate mousse."

"Whoa, fancy! I'll talk to you later then." Val hung up, amazed at how cheerful she had become. She pressed number two on speed-dial for Toby.

"Guess what," Val said.

"Your angel came," Toby answered promptly.

"Can't I surprise anyone?" Val groaned. "Lulu guessed, too."

"What does she look like? Oh, I'll never forget the first sight of Serena on the ceiling," Toby gushed. "And the time she played the piano and helped me dance *The Firebird*—"

Val interrupted. "Will you let me tell you about *my* angel?"

"Sorry," Toby apologized. "I get so carried away when I think of Serena."

"I was carried away, all right!" Val giggled. "Amber and I flew."

"No!" Toby said, astonished.

"Yes. And she's very smart. She's going to help solve the mystery with us."

"All right!" Toby exclaimed. "But right now, Val, I'm on my way to see if I can find Felicia. I have a few questions to ask her about her whereabouts yesterday afternoon. I'll watch her expressions closely. They always give criminals away."

"Good luck," Val said.

Val hit number three on speed-dial. This time she didn't ask, she simply blurted out the news. "My angel came!"

"Way to go!" Rachel cheered. "I'm so glad for you. Did your angel land upside down like mine?"

"No! We both landed right side up." And then she told Rachel about her flight and about Amber's questioning and investigation of the mystery.

"It's all going to work out, I just know it." Rachel's voice sounded confident. "I'm on my way to meet Toby. We're going over to see Felicia."

"So Sherlock Antonio told me. Good luck, Rachel, and thanks," said Val.

"No sweat. Hey, now that all four members of the Angel Club have met their angels, we absolutely have to have a party," added Rachel.

"I can't think about that right now," Val said. "We have to save my dad's newspaper and all the town's businesses, remember?"

"Of course. And I hear Toby on the stairs. We'll have this caper cracked in no time, just you wait!"

After Val put down the phone, she thought about Amber and her Angel Club friends for a while. Maybe her life was still perfect after all.

Suddenly Tracy came running into Val's room, breaking her reverie. "Who were you talking to before? I heard some other voice."

"It was the radio," Val said quickly.

"But the radio isn't on," said Tracy.

"Um, that's because I turned it off, smartie," replied Val.

"Uh-uh!" Tracy shook her head. "I think you were talking to an angel. My friend Zena told me that angels come here when someone is in trouble. And I think you were talking to your angel."

Val stared at Tracy with her mouth open. What could she say? "You're right, Tracy. I was talking to my angel."

"I *knew* it!" Tracy grinned. "Oh, Mom wants to see you downstairs. Maybe she needs an angel, too."

"We'll see what we can do about that, pumpkin, okay?" said Val, and she squeezed Tracy's shoulder.

Val hurried downstairs to see if her mother and stepfather had learned anything new or important about the investigation. She found Mrs. McCall in the den, typing away furiously on the computer.

"I'm faxing apologies to every one of my clients," she explained to Val, "though I don't think it will make much difference once they read that I add 20 percent onto their airfares for myself down at the travel agency."

"Oh, I feel so awful . . ." Val said, her eyes welling up with tears again. "I'll get started on my apology for the newspaper right away."

"I know you feel bad." Mrs. McCall gazed up at her. "We all do, but we'll live through this thing one way or another. Val, you know that your dad and I love you, no matter what."

Val was grateful to hear those words, especially just then. She felt her courage rising. Her parents had always come through for her before. Now, it was Val's turn to come through for them.

That same morning, just a mile away, in the McWithers mansion, the emotional weather was also stormy, but considerably colder than at the McCall house.

"Felicia, you're late for brunch again." Mrs. McWithers scowled. "You know your father prefers that you finish eating before he comes to the table." She was at the large dining-room table, pouring coffee out of a silver coffeepot.

"I'm sorry," Felicia said.

"And you've forgotten to comb your hair," her mother added.

"No I didn't," Felicia retorted. "I've combed it twice already." She nervously smoothed down her long, straight blond hair.

"It's important to always look your best," Mrs.

McWithers reminded her. "After all, our family must set the standards for the entire town."

"Must we?" muttered Felicia under her breath, but her mother ignored her.

"Good morning, dear," Mrs. McWithers said brightly to Mr. McWithers as he strode in. He wore a finely tailored dark suit and was carrying a Gucci briefcase.

"I have a business meeting after breakfast," he explained.

"You always have a business meeting," Felicia said.

Her father glared at her through his thin horn-rimmed glasses. "If I didn't tend to business, you wouldn't have all the good things in life."

"Who asked for them?" Felicia retorted.

"Don't be rude to your father," Mrs. McWithers said edgily. "By the way," she added, while buttering her croissant, "I'm taking you to Madame Fontana for your first singing lesson next week. Ballet wasn't your strong point, but I wouldn't be surprised if a prima donna diva was hiding in you."

Felicia's face was a picture of misery. "What's a prima donna diva?" she asked.

"Why, an opera star, Felicia. You know, *Carmen*, *Madame Butterfly*."

"I prefer Pearl Jam," responded Felicia.

Mrs. McWithers ignored her daughter and picked up the *Angel Corners Gazette* that her maid had brought in. "Oh dear me!" she said in mock horror. "Someone has written a simply scandalous column. Listen to this, dear," she ordered her husband:

"Beware all travelers! Angel Corners Travel Agency pockets 20 percent of its ticket prices and sells cruises on ships that do not exist!"

Mrs. McWithers cackled with pleasure. "That should put that smug Mrs. McCall out of business! And—oh!—you should see what they're saying about Mayor Witty and—"

"Let me see that!" Mr. McWithers seized the paper and searched for his own name.

Halfway down the column, sandwiched between the Laundromat with dryers that spewed lint and the Sweet Shop that used fake maple syrup on their pancakes, was one short question: "And how does McWithers make all his money?" He read it out loud, followed by silence. His wife and daughter held their breath. Then, after a moment, Mr. McWithers's loud laugh filled the dining room. "Wouldn't they like to know?"

Felicia coughed nervously. She had lost her appetite. "Dad, you promised to go horseback riding with me today, remember?"

"Too busy," he muttered.

"But this is the third time you've cancelled. Why do you keep all those horses if you never ride them?"

"Investments, of course, but don't tell the *Gazette!*" Her father laughed at his own joke and took a bite of croissant. "We'll go riding another time."

"That's what you always say."

He shrugged and resumed reading the paper.

Felicia got up from the table and dashed upstairs to her room, slamming the door. "Nobody cares a hair about me! I'm going for a walk." She grabbed her French raincoat and went out.

Her appetite returned the moment she left her house, so she headed to the Sweet Shop for a late breakfast. But no sooner was she sitting in a booth and biting into her first pancake, than Sylvie and Andrea—friends of the Angel Club—came in. "Now that my dad has a job," Felicia heard Andrea saying, "I can buy lots more treats—" Andrea's voice fell when she saw Felicia. "Um, did you read Val's column?" she asked.

"I can't be bothered." Felicia shrugged.

"I don't believe that," Sylvie said, and gently elbowed her friend.

"Yes, I don't believe that, either," Andrea said, her voice getting stronger. "In fact, *we* think maybe *you* wrote it! Val would never do such a thing, but you would."

"Well, aren't you getting brave, to speak to me that way," Felicia said sarcastically.

"I am!" Andrea said proudly. "I'll never let you push me around again." She stuck her tongue out at Felicia. Felicia remembered when Andrea followed her around like a puppy dog, doing anything Felicia told her just so she could have a friend.

Andrea and Sylvie sat in a booth in the far corner. Occasionally, as she ate her pancakes, Felicia heard the two good friends giggling. They had completely forgotten about her.

But when Felicia stood up to leave, she noticed that Andrea and Sylvie stopped talking. She would not give them the satisfaction of looking in their direction, but gathered her purse and headed straight out the door.

No sooner was she on her way home than she spied Toby Antonio and Rachel Summers coming her way. When they saw her, they quickened their pace.

Toby came storming toward her.

"Did you write this column?" she shouted at Felicia, shaking the *Gazette* in the air.

"What column?" Felicia asked.

"Don't pretend you don't know." Toby glared. "The whole town knows. And I'm warning you, Felicia, if I find out that you did this, I'm going to break every bone in your body."

smart enough. She's too much of a goody-goody any-way. Ha! I bet the whole town is after her! Now, she can see what it's like when nobody likes you.

Felicia dipped her fingers into her jewelry box and went on reading the column. *This should definitely rip apart the Angel Club. Each of the members and their families are nicely insulted. And Andrea's father, too. Good thing my dad didn't get upset!*

Sighing, Felicia slipped on an emerald ring. It was so valuable her parents had forbidden her to wear it anywhere except in the house.

"You are so pretty," Felicia crooned. "It's a shame I can't wear you around town and make everyone sick with envy."

Suddenly Felicia heard a giggle. "I'm better than any old ring," came a voice from the emerald on her finger.

Felicia stared at her hand, which started to shake ever so slightly. *Am I losing my mind? I could swear that voice came out of my ring.*

"Now, now, no swearing," said the voice.

Felicia's eyes grew wide as the emerald ring began slowly twirling around. It eased itself off her finger. The ring hovered in the air and then began to grow bigger and bigger. A face emerged out of a swirl of green and a set of wings—green wings—and then an entire tiny angel—with green eyes and green hair.

"Hello, Felicia." The creature took out a flute from behind a pigtail and tooted a few notes. "Ta da! I am Emerald, your guardian angel!" she announced.

Felicia stared at her coldly. "Guardian angels do not exist."

"I do so exist." Emerald's green eyes flashed. "And I took a great risk coming to help you, so a little appreciation would be nice."

Felicia kept glaring. "I know what you are. You're a magician my father hired. He loves to spend money on stunts to impress people. Well, *I* am not impressed."

"*I am not a stunt!*" Emerald lost her temper. "I came to you because I love you!"

Felicia's expression grew quizzical. "My father's stunts never say nice things like that."

Emerald flew over to Felicia's bed. "I'll always love you, no matter what."

"What about my ring?" asked Felicia. "I want it back!"

"There it is, on your finger, silly," said Emerald.

Felicia looked at the green sparkle on her finger and gasped. "You must be an angel!" And then she fainted dead away.

5

Felicia's Angel

E merald murmured into Felicia's ear. "It's going to be all right. I know I'm an enormous surprise . . . and you never even asked for me . . . but I decided to come, anyway. You see, Florinda mentioned that there are some really difficult cases . . ."

Slowly Felicia opened her eyes again. "Who's a difficult case? And who's Florinda?" She glared. "I can't believe that dumb Angel Club is right—angels do exist." She studied Emerald closely. "You look . . . um . . . sort of scruffy."

"Really?" Emerald was hurt, though she tried not to show it.

"My mother says it's important always to have a perfect appearance."

Emerald tried to ignore that remark. She reached over to stroke Felicia's hair, but the girl moved away. "Wait a second!" she asked suspiciously. "Who sent you?"

"*I* sent me! I already told you." shouted Emerald. "I'm beginning to lose my temper." She opened her wings and flew to the windowsill. She perched there, facing away from Felicia, seized her flute from behind her ear, and began to play. The music rose up dangerously high and then fell down the scales, the notes playing tag with each other. "Ah, I feel calmer, now," said Emerald as she put her flute back behind her ear. Then she took a deep breath and flew back to Felicia.

"Whoever you are, you certainly can fly," Felicia commented. "*And* play the flute."

"Thank you." Emerald smiled. "Now, please tell me how I can help you."

"I don't need any help." Felicia began glaring again. "We McWithers don't need help from anyone. Daddy says that all the time."

Emerald quickly counted to 4 million to calm herself.

"Felicia," said Emerald in a big-sister tone of voice, which Felicia had never heard before, "I think you and your family need a lot of help. Take brunch this morning. Was that a pleasant experience? Your dad doesn't want you eating while he's eating because you'll disturb him. And your mom says you hadn't combed your hair when you *had* combed your hair, because she wasn't paying attention to you. And what's all that nonsense about voice lessons? You wouldn't like that any more than you liked ballet! And you say you don't need help? Honey, if you don't, who does?"

Felicia tried to explain. "It's just that I'm not very good at anything and they want me to be better."

"I'm not so sure about that," Emerald scowled. "They want you to be better at what *they* want you to be. But what about you? For example, you write a pretty mean newspaper column—"

"*I did not write that column!* Why does everyone think I wrote it?" shouted Felicia, though Emerald was sitting quite close enough to hear.

"You didn't? Hmmm, are you sure?" asked Emerald gently.

"Of course I'm sure." A light went on in Felicia's head. "Hey, I bet that old Angel Club sent you over here to get me to confess! Well, I didn't write that stupid article, and if I had I would have done it even better. I'd have written about the Angel Club believing in angels, and they'd all be put away in the loony bin. So go back and tell that to Ms. Toby Antonio and the others!" Felicia turned away so Emerald could not see her tears of disappointment.

"I *am* your angel," said Emerald softly, "and I really want to help you. Come on, try to trust me."

Felicia shook her head. "You just want to get my hopes up, like Daddy. He makes all kinds of promises, but he breaks every single one of them."

"Please, Felicia," said her angel, her voice strained by emotion, "please trust me, just a little."

"Why? Why should I?"

"Because I came here to help you!"

"No." Felicia's eyes filled with tears again. "Go away," she cried, and buried her head in her pillow. She would not listen to another word.

Emerald was at a total loss. *If Amber can do this, why can't I? Serena, Merrie, and Celeste all managed it. What am I doing wrong?* Emerald flew out the window and decided to take a walk around Angel Corners, to get a feel for this strange place called earth.

Despite all the turmoil over Val's column in the *Angel Corners Gazette,* Main Street was quiet. Emerald dawdled as she walked, looking into the windows of each store she passed, and nodding to each passerby. She didn't notice the odd looks she was getting from people on the street until she heard a woman whisper to her husband, "Kids these days! Can you imagine our Stephanie coming home with green hair?" A few moments later a boy on a bicycle called out to Emerald, "Nice costume, but Halloween is over!"

Oh my, Emerald thought, *I forgot to change!* People were stopping to stare and point.

At just that moment a tall young black man stepped out of the Angel Corners Celestial Bookstore. "Excuse me, but perhaps you should come into my store before you cause more of a stir on the street."

"Oh, thank you," said Emerald, following him inside. He flipped the OPEN sign on the door to read CLOSED.

"Folks around here may pride themselves on their tradition of angel sightings, but very few would appreciate coming face-to-face with an angel on a Saturday morning stroll."

"So you recognize me!" cried Emerald enthusiastically.

"Oh yes," said the bookstore owner knowingly. "My name is Derek Weatherby. And yours?"

"I'm called Emerald," the angel said, still grinning from having been recognized.

"Emerald. That's a suitable name for you, isn't it? But, let me ask you a question, Emerald."

"Okay," she said.

"Does anyone know you are here? From up there, I mean."

Emerald was taken aback. She had expected the

man to ask if she could really fly or whether she could make him rich or what it was like in heaven. "What do you mean?"

"Well, I know a thing or two about angels and how things work up there and it seems to me that you are a bit young to be down here on your own." Derek spoke softly, as if he were talking to a child. "Shouldn't you have changed yourself so you looked like an everyday mortal, to walk the streets of an everyday town?"

"Oh, that," said Emerald, laughing nervously. "I just forgot. Of course they know I'm here. I was sent."

"Uh-huh," Derek murmured, nodding his head.

"But I really can't talk about it, you being a mortal. This is angels' business." *Who is this man?* she thought. *I have to get out of here before Florinda finds me!* "And I really must be going now. I have so much to do. Thank you, Mr. Weatherby, for rescuing me from the streets—"

"Call me Derek," the man said.

My, noticed Emerald, *he is good-looking, and with a voice to melt butter. Wait until I tell the angels about him!*

"Derek, I really must be going," Emerald said again. "Do you mind if I change in your book stacks?"

"Be my guest," Derek answered.

Val McCall, Ace Reporter?

A moment later a young woman walked out of the fiction section wearing a nice pair of black jeans with an emerald-green sweater and matching suede boots. Her hair was tied up in a paisley turban, not a green strand showing. She didn't exactly look like an everyday mortal, but she looked awfully pretty. In her hand she held a book.

"I think I'll take this one, Derek," she said with a smile.

Derek rang up the sale. "Nice choice: *Rachel, Meet Your Angel!* We sell a lot of copies here."

"Thank you, Derek," said Emerald saucily and turned to leave.

"Listen, Emerald," said Derek, "if you find you need some help . . . if you get in a spot of trouble . . . remember, I'll be here to help you."

Emerald winked at him and walked out the door, swinging the CLOSED sign back to OPEN.

As soon as she was gone, Derek sat down on the stool behind his counter. *Whew! I wonder if Florinda knows she's here.*

CHAPTER

6

On the Sweet Shop Steps

That evening, Emerald was walking down the path from the top of Angel Falls when she heard a noise above her. It was Amber.

"Oh, Amber," said Emerald, startled. "Hello."

"And exactly what are you doing here?" asked Amber as she landed squarely in front of Emerald, blocking the path.

"Aren't you even going to say hello or how pleasantly surprised you are to see me?" asked Emerald. "After all, I did come down here to help you out."

"Help me out?" Amber looked puzzled. "Does Florinda know you are here?"

"Doesn't Florinda, the Queen of the Angels, know everything?"

Val McCall, Ace Reporter?

Amber paused to consider Emerald's question. *Florinda is supposed to know everything, that's true, so she must know that Emerald is here.* "Well," said Amber, "since you are here, have you discovered anything to help Val out of her mess? I've come up empty-handed so far."

"All I know for sure is that Felicia McWithers didn't write that column," said Emerald. "I spent most of the day with her, and I know she didn't do it."

"Hm," Amber hummed. "I was pretty sure she was the culprit. But now it looks like it was either Zeb Burgess or an unknown third party."

Emerald nodded in agreement.

"Listen, Emerald, I have to work on Val's shyness about talking to Zeb. She has to talk to him about this! He took an extra-long time leaving the newspaper office, and that gave him plenty of time to rewrite the article. Maybe it would help if you spend some time at Zeb's house tonight and see what you think of him."

Emerald answered sharply. "I do have other things to do, you know." She certainly didn't want to be under Amber's supervision. She wanted to get back to helping Felicia—if Felicia would let her.

"Oh, I *am* sorry. I didn't think you'd mind helping me. Maybe I should fly up and ask Florinda to send someone besides you."

"On second thought," piped up Emerald quickly, "I wouldn't mind getting to know this Zeb Burgess. I hear he's really cute. I'll tell you what: I'll help you out if you forget about telling Florinda you ran into me here, okay?"

"I think we understand each other," said Amber. Emerald nodded and, sprouting her wings, flew away as fast as she could.

As Amber turned toward Val's house, she was thoughtful. *Did Florinda send Emerald without telling me or is she here as a runaway angel? Either way, I sure could use some help!*

The McCall family was at dinner, but no one had much of an appetite. "I spoke to everyone who works at the *Gazette* today," Mr. McCall was saying. "But they all deny writing that column. I don't know what to do next."

"I'm sure none of your employees would do this," Mrs. McCall assured him. "They have almost as much at stake as we do."

"Maybe this is a computer virus or something," offered Val.

"Not likely." Mr. McCall speared a piece of broccoli. "No virus can be this fiendishly clever. It has to be someone who knows the town from A to Z in order to insult each business in just its most vulnerable spots."

"The Angel Club hasn't found any clues either," Val said. "We've narrowed down our list of suspects. Toby and Rachel are going to talk to Felicia McWithers, and tomorrow Lulu and I are supposed to interview Zeb Burgess."

"Now look, honey," said Mrs. McCall, "I don't want you and your friends to go poking around too much. The town is mad enough already. Your investigation could make matters worse."

"But we have to do *something* to help," cried Val.

"Listen," Mr. McCall interrupted, "I spoke with Sheriff Perkins today. He offered to help with the investigation officially. It seems this could be seen as a case of breaking and entering, not to mention outright theft of your article, and libel. We're meeting at the *Gazette* office in the morning. Val, perhaps you should join us."

"Gosh, Dad, do you really want to get the sheriff involved?" asked Val.

"It's not up to me, honey. A crime has been committed. Personally, I welcome the help. He can do a lot more with an official investigation than you, I, or the Angel Club."

"I don't know about *that*," came a voice from near the ceiling that only Val could hear. It was Amber, and was Val ever glad to see her.

"May I please be excused?" asked Val.

"Yes, you may," said her mother. "If you don't

have much homework to do, I'd like you to keep working on your apology for the paper."

"Okay, Mom," said Val and hurried from the dining room to her bedroom, where Amber was already waiting.

"Val, I'm afraid I don't have much news." Amber began. "The town is definitely in shock over this column. Stores and businesses are pulling their ads, people are calling their lawyers, and Mayor Witty is even thinking about cancelling the tourist week-end." Amber got the bad news out all at once.

Val slumped on her couch. The crackling fire was gone, the hot chocolate was gone, but Amber was still there. Val looked at her angel with bright eyes. "What can we do? I want to catch the culprit before Sheriff Perkins does. It's my responsibility!"

"I know it's been a hard day for you, Val," Amber said softly. "And I don't mean to be critical, but there is one important job you haven't done yet."

"What?" Val asked. "I'm almost finished with my apology for the paper."

"I'll give you a hint. His initials are Z.B."

"Zeb?" Val blushed bright red. "Zeb would never do something as awful as rewriting my column."

"Who said he would?" Amber replied calmly. "But you did promise the Angel Club that you—and

Lulu—would talk to him. You want to do a complete investigation, don't you? Zeb was at the office on Friday. He may have a clue you can use."

"That's true," Val agreed. "But questioning Zeb? I can hardly look at him without stuttering. And even if I could talk to him, he'd get mad at me for suspecting him of such a horrible thing."

"Val," said Amber gently, "you've got to be a little braver. Why are you so scared of offending Zeb?"

"I want him to like me!" Val protested.

"Is he going to like you any better if you *never* talk to him?" asked Amber. "Val, your stepfather's business is at stake."

"Of course. I know what I'll do, Amber. I *will* go talk to Zeb. But first I'll study his videotape some more. Then I'll write a list of questions, and then I'll practice them with Lulu, and then . . ."

Amber groaned. "That sounds like a five-year plan!"

"I'm sorry. I'm doing the best I can," Val cried.

"Val, dear," said Amber very gently, "I really believe you can do better than that."

"Okay, okay." Val nodded. "I'll call Lulu, and we'll go and see Zeb tomorrow."

"That sounds like a fine idea," said Amber with an angelic smile. "Don't hesitate to call me." And Amber disappeared, leaving behind a lovely birch fire and a mug of hot chocolate.

Amber met Emerald hovering over Zeb's house. "What's the report, Emerald?"

"Boring! All Zeb does is lift weights and read magazines. Before bedtime, he wrestled with his older brother, Zeke, and lost. Boys!"

Meanwhile, Val called Lulu.

Lulu answered the phone. "Hey, stranger."

"How did you know it was me?" asked Val.

"Who else calls me every night before bedtime to tell me about her day—except when I call her first?"

"Of course!" Val slapped her head in pretend disgust at her forgetfulness. "But tonight I have a special request."

"Shoot, pardner," said Lulu in her best John Wayne imitation, which was pretty bad.

"I want you to meet me at the Sweet Shop tomorrow morning. Zeb has breakfast there every Sunday, and I promised Amber I would question him tomorrow. I need all the help I can get. Will you come with me?"

"Of course, Val. You *are* being brave," said Lulu admiringly.

"I have no choice. Listen to this: Sheriff Perkins is starting his own investigation tomorrow morning. We've *got* to find out who did it first."

"I'm with you all the way. But I have to hang up now. Dad and Sally are watching *The Day the Earth*

Stood Still and they said I could stay up and watch it with them."

"Just be up in time for breakfast!" said Val.

"Right!" Lulu said, and hung up the phone.

Val spent another hour sipping piping hot, angelic, hot chocolate, watching the fire burn down, and putting the final touches on her apology.

As they walked to the Sweet Shop the next morning, Lulu told Val she thought her angel would have found the culprit by now.

Val flared up. "My angel is wonderful. Don't you dare criticize her."

"I'm not." Lulu backed off. "Chill out, Val!"

"Okay, okay," said Val as she neared the Sweet Shop. "I am just a little nervous."

"Right," said Lulu comfortingly. "That's why I'm here, remember?"

Just then, Val recognized a couple of her classmates and their parents coming out the door. "Oh-oh," she said to Lulu, "let's get out of here." But they weren't fast enough.

Sam Eisenstein poked Val. "My dad's suing your dad for what you said about his pet supply store. You know very well we don't recycle old cat food."

"I didn't—" Val began.

Sam wouldn't listen. He scowled and walked away.

"Some nerve you have!" Jimmy Nordstrom came running up to her. "My family's shoe repair does not use cardboard instead of leather heels!"

"I'm sorry, Jimmy. You know I didn't write that," Val began.

But Jimmy wouldn't listen to Val, either.

Val felt awful. She felt everyone staring at her angrily. "They're making me feel like an outcast, someone *nobody* likes—like Felicia."

Just then the Burgess family came out.

"Here's your chance, Val," prompted Lulu.

"How do I look?" Val asked, panicking.

"You look great," Lulu said. "Go for it."

Val was wearing a forest-green dress with a lace collar that made her feel somewhat brave and also pretty. She walked up to the Burgesses as calmly as she could.

"Good morning, Mr. and Mrs. Burgess. I hope you are well," said Val.

"Val, I'm so glad to see you," said Mrs. Burgess. "Excuse me for being so blunt, but how is your family holding up under all of this nonsense over that newspaper article?"

Val blushed to the very roots of her hair.

"We're managing, thank you." Val paused and took a deep breath. "Would you mind if I talked to Zeb for a minute?"

It was Zeb's turn to blush.

"Of course not," said Mrs. Burgess. "We'll just be getting on home." She nudged her husband, and they walked off.

Zeb and Val both stared at the ground for a whole minute before Val summoned her courage to speak.

"Zeb," she began, and instantly felt her throat dry up, "did you mess with my column for the *Gazette?* You were the only other person at the office on Friday when I was there. . . . Did *you* do it?" Val sounded like she was close to tears.

"No, Val, I didn't!" Zeb answered. But Val noticed he didn't look her in the eye when he said it. "And that's just what I'm going to tell Sheriff Perkins."

"Sheriff Perkins?" asked Val, aghast.

"He called this morning, and said I have to get down to his office later. Look, Val, I have to go." Zeb hurried away without looking back.

"Well?" asked Lulu after Zeb had disappeared. "You finally talked to him! What did he say?"

"He said he didn't do it," responded Val. "And I believe him."

"What did Zeb say about why it took him so long to leave the office then?" Lulu prodded.

"I didn't ask him."

"What?"

"He *said* he didn't do it! And that's good enough for me," Val answered curtly.

"Yeah," agreed Lulu, "he's too dumb to lie."

"Lulu Bliss!" Val glared at her best friend.

"I'm sorry! That didn't come out right," Lulu apologized. "What I mean is that Zeb isn't the sneaky type. With Zeb, what you see is what you get." Lulu shut her mouth before she got into more trouble.

"Of course." Val smiled, thinking about her first conversation with the love of her life. "I told you he's too adorable to do anything that awful."

Just then, Felicia and her parents drove by in their brand-new red Rolls-Royce.

"It's interesting, isn't it," Lulu asked Val, "that none of her father's businesses was insulted in your column—I mean—*the* column. Not the bank. Or the insurance company. Or his stables. There was just that little question about how he made his money. It is odd, Val, isn't it?"

"Toby called me last night to say that she and Rachel had questioned Ms. Fancy-pants Mc-Withers," said Val. "Of course, she denied it."

"Don't be fooled," warned Lulu. "Once a Felicia, always a Felicia!"

After a somber, drizzly afternoon of homework, Val finally asked Amber if she would come and talk to her. No sooner were the whispered words out of her mouth than Val felt a pair of angelic hands gently rubbing her shoulders.

"Oh, Amber," said Val, "I don't know what to do. I talked to Zeb this morning, and of course he didn't write that nasty column, but Sheriff Perkins had him down at the station for questioning. It's too terrible, and it's all my fault!"

"No, dear," said Amber. "Your only fault was not reading over your article before sending it to the printer. You really can't take the blame for whoever changed it. Everyone has choices to make about how they act and react. You must remember that you can be responsible only for your own choices."

While Amber talked, Val's tears dried, and she felt a weight lift from her shoulders. "Amber, you make me feel so much better."

"That's part of my job," said Amber. "I think you've also made yourself feel better by writing your apology. May I see it?"

"Of course," said Val, and she picked up a sheet of paper from her desk. It was printed out perfectly pristine:

To the businesspeople and residents of Angel Corners:

Last week a horrible column was printed by mistake under my name. I didn't write it, but I did not read over my work before sending it to the printer. Somehow, that insulting list of lies was printed in its place.

I am very sorry for all the pain and anger I have caused. Angel Corners is my hometown, and I love everything about it. I would never want to say anything negative about it. Again, I apologize for this terrible mistake.

Sincerely yours,
Valentine McCall

"Very nicely written," said Amber. "And it took an amazing amount of courage to say all of this in print."

"Do you really think so?" asked Val.

"I do. And I earned an A+ in Advanced Angelic Diplomacy. I know about tricky situations."

Val giggled—for the first time in days, it seemed.

"I think I'm ready to show this to my parents now," said Val.

"I imagine it will make them very proud." Amber smiled at Val. "I think it is perfect."

"Okay," said Val as she walked toward the bedroom door. "Here goes . . ."

Amber fluttered around outside the McCalls' study window, watching while Val showed her parents the letter. They read it gravely, then raised their sparkling eyes to each other before wrapping Val in a tremendous hug.

7

ZAP!

Before Ms. Fisher began the school day, she made an announcement. "I just wanted to tell Val how sorry I am about the trouble over her column in the *Angel Corners Gazette.* I don't believe you could have written such terrible things, Val. And I expect the members of this class to react similarly. I will not allow this episode to disrupt our lessons."

"Thank you," Val said gratefully.

Jimmy Nordstrom spoke up. "On the way to school today, Zeb Burgess told me that if he finds the culprit, he's going to zap him."

Val's heart skipped a beat at the mention of Zeb's name. Then she smiled, imagining him zapping whoever did it, thus saving her reputation like a white knight.

In the middle of math, Val felt a tap on her shoulder. Someone was handing her a note. She read it quickly:

Did you notice that Zeb loves to say "zap"? And the person who wrote that column said "zap"! How do you feel about that?—Lulu.

Zeb couldn't have done it! I wouldn't have a crush on him if he were horrible enough to do something like that. Besides, he said he didn't do it! Val just had to believe him. Then there came another tap. This time the note was from Rachel:

Zap! Zap! I hate to say this, but do you think maybe Zeb wrote your column? He's always zapping everything and everybody!—Rachel.

Lots of people say zap, *not just Zeb.* Val told herself. She glanced over at Felicia. *Maybe she wrote the column to get both me* and *Zeb into trouble?*

"Val, would you please open your math book?" Ms. Fisher's voice interrupted her.

"Sorry."

"Felicia." Ms. Fisher turned to her. "Would you

come up to the board and solve this fraction problem?"

"I can't," Felicia answered quickly.

"You are going to flunk math if you don't catch up to the rest of the class," Ms. Fisher warned her. "And you know how upset that will make your parents."

"I know . . . but I just don't get it," Felicia mumbled.

"Pssst, Felicia!"

Felicia gazed down and saw Emerald seated on her math book.

"Why don't you ask Ms. Fisher to give you a quick lesson after school?"

Felicia was startled. She had almost convinced herself that her angel wasn't real, but here she was again—in miniature!

Quickly, Felicia stood her book up to hide the little green-haired angel. "Ms. Fisher isn't going to stay after school to help me. She can't be bothered."

"Come on," Emerald insisted. "Trust someone just this once. I bet she'll say yes."

Thinking about the scene her mother would make at the sight of an F in math, Felicia raised her hand. "Um . . . Ms. Fisher," she said shyly. "Could you explain fractions to me just for a minute or two after school? Maybe that would help."

"Of course, I will." Ms. Fisher nodded. "I'm glad you asked for help."

Felicia smiled. *Hmm,* she began thinking, *Maybe I should take Emerald's advice more often. Maybe she is on my side.* She glanced down behind her math book, but Emerald was gone.

Oh, please come back! Felicia thought frantically.

"I am here." Her angel waved at her, from a perch on top of the wall map of the United States. Emerald was about the size of Alaska. "I'm staying with you, Felicia. You can count on that." She threw Felicia a big kiss.

Felicia was so pleased, she flushed a happy red.

Val noticed it. *Felicia's looking awfully cheerful for someone who's just been told she's flunking math.*

When class was over, Lulu grabbed Val's hand. "We have to have an Angel Club meeting right now!"

After all four girls were settled in the lunchroom with pizza slices, Lulu said, "Felicia looks much too happy. She must have done it!"

"But how can we prove it?" Rachel said.

"You can think about that," said Toby, "while I go and ask Zeb why he says 'zap' a lot just like the person who wrote your column."

"He's at the corner table," Val said, "But he did not do it!"

"Funny, how you noticed that," Toby snickered,

"and how can you be so sure?" She got up and pretended to slam-dunk a basketball while she did. Toby liked to be dramatic.

The Angel Club watched as Toby asked Zeb questions in rapid-fire order. Zeb answered them calmly, cracking his knuckles as he spoke. Toby cringed every time she heard CRA-ACK!

In a few minutes, she was back.

"So what did he say?" Val asked quickly.

"He said he didn't do it."

Val allowed herself a satisfying smirk.

"But what about the zapping stuff?" Lulu persisted.

"Zeb told me it's a family joke." Toby paused for a sip of soda. "You see, his dad's name is Zoran and his older brother is Zeke. They have contests to come up with new z-words. Zap is Zeb's newest."

"So now we're right back where we started," groaned Lulu. "No suspects."

"Not 'no suspects,' " said Rachel as she nodded in the direction of the ponytailed, silver-braceleted, smiling Felicia McWithers.

8

Run!

After school that day, Val picked up Tracy from her class and went to check at the newspaper office to see if the investigation had borne any fruit.

"No," Mr. McCall said. "And if we don't find that person soon, I'll have to shut down the paper. Everyone has pulled their advertisements and I've been fielding lawyers' calls all day. The libel suits will bankrupt me."

Val trudged home. Tracy walked with her, bouncing a ball in time with their footsteps. "I wish we could find out who did this," Tracy said.

"Stop that! It's getting on my nerves," Val snapped.

Val McCall, Ace Reporter?

"You're so mean to me lately!" Tracy yelled, and ran ahead, still bouncing her ball.

"I'm sorry," Val called after her. As soon as she got home, she heard the phone ringing.

"It's Toby. Remember the relay race the Angel Club is running in school? We need to practice for it. Can you meet us right now?"

Val exploded. "Toby, how can you think of a race when my dad may lose his newspaper?"

"Running will help us think," Toby declared. "Exercise releases endorphins in your brain. The chemicals make you feel better, so you think better. And don't you dare yell at me, Val. *I'm* not the one who got us into this trouble!"

"Okay, I'm sorry. If you think it might help, I'll change into my sweats and be right there."

"Good! See you." Toby hung up. Val changed her clothes and left the house. She passed Andrea and Sylvie on Main Street. They seemed startled to see her.

"We're on our way to practice gymnastics," Sylvie said, her face flushed as if she'd been caught at something. "The gym teacher says Andrea and I have flexible joints, whatever that means."

"It means a lot!" Val said. "I was terrible at gymnastics."

"Well," said Sylvie, "we gotta go!" And the

two of them ran off, faster than rabbits. Val could not help smiling. Both Andrea and Sylvie had become so much more confident in the past few months.

Suddenly, not two steps away, Val saw a yellow Post-it stuck to a tree. In purple printing, it read: WHOEVER WROTE VAL MCCALL'S COLUMN BETTER CONFESS! WE KNOW WHO YOU ARE!

"I wonder who wrote that," Val said.

While Val hurried to Toby's house to meet the Angel Club, Felicia was walking home, alone. Well, not exactly alone. Emerald was casually hovering around. Felicia saw the Post-it note, too. "Uh-oh," she gasped. "I wonder who knows about—"

Emerald's ears perked up so much, her flute fell to the ground. Quickly, Felicia changed the subject. "Emerald, I can understand the math problems now. Ms. Fisher stayed after school with me for twenty minutes to explain them."

"I know. I was there," Emerald reminded her, but at that moment her mind was on what Felicia had started to say when she saw the yellow Post-it.

Felicia giggled. "You know I thought Ms. Fisher hated me. But she doesn't."

A shout from across the street interrupted Felicia's thoughts of Ms. Fisher. Toby was holding a stopwatch and urging Rachel, Lulu, and Val to get ready for their race. "If we beat our record, we'll win the class race."

Rachel, Lulu, and even Val responded with a communal high five amid their cheers.

Emerald asked, "Felicia, do you play any sports?"

"No. Mom says it's unladylike."

"Really?"

Toby handed a wand to Rachel. "Ready! Set! Go!" she shouted, and Rachel began running down the block.

"Look at that expression on Rachel's face," Emerald said. "She's having a wonderful time! And Toby, Val, and Lulu can't wait for their turns. They're jogging in place while they wait."

"Oh, them," Felicia groaned. "They're so silly."

"I don't think so," Emerald insisted. "Up in the heavenly spheres, we're always racing around. How about a quick run with me right now?"

"I can't." Felicia shook her head. "What if I fall and break a leg or something? Mom says that I'm too clumsy."

"I don't think you're clumsy at all." Emerald's eyes flashed angrily. "Not if you have the right equipment." Emerald waved her flute over Felicia's shoes, and—just like in *The Wizard of Oz*—her shoes instantly changed, only in this case to ruby-red running shoes.

"But you'll have to take those bracelets off," Emerald said. "They'll make a terrible racket while you run."

"I will not." Felicia looked horrified. "I feel naked without them."

"Okay, okay," Emerald agreed. "Now I'm going to start running slowly, and you just keep up with me. Okay?"

"All right." Felicia began a light jog behind Emerald, whose feet, of course, barely touched the ground.

"Now a little faster," Emerald called out.

On the other side of the street, the Angel Club continued running their relay race. Lulu was handing the baton to Toby. "Go! Go! Go!" she yelled.

Toby raced like the wind, her long legs taking enormous strides. As Felicia watched her, she suddenly stopped. "This is ridiculous," Felicia told Emerald. "I'll never be as good as her."

"So what?" Emerald answered. "Who says you have to be? All you have to do is have a good time. Come on. Keep going. You were really loosening up."

"No!" Felicia said firmly. "If I can't do anything well, I shouldn't do it at all. That's what Mom says. I don't know why I let you talk me into this!"

"Felicia," Emerald said softly, "have you ever thought that your mother might be wrong about some things? Her attitude takes all the fun out of life."

Felicia looked surprised. "What are you talking about? I have lots of fun."

"Like what?" Emerald challenged her.

Felicia's eyes grew sad. "Um . . . er . . ." She thought for a moment. Then she grew frustrated and glared at Emerald. "How I have fun is none of your business! Now, are you going to give me back my shoes or not?"

"Okay, okay." Emerald sighed, holding Felicia's loafers in front of her. "But first you'll have to catch me!" And off ran Emerald.

Felicia didn't hesitate. "Why you no-good little tooth fairy! Give me back my shoes!"

And the chase was on, up and down the sidewalk, cutting across lawns, running around houses until both Emerald and Felicia collapsed back where they had started, in a fit of laughter.

As she and Emerald lay on the grass giggling, they saw the Angel Club jumping around, slapping each other on the back.

"We did it!" Toby was shouting. "We broke our record. Yay!"

"The Angel Club will win the race! Yes!" All four girls exchanged high fives.

"Big deal," said Felicia, suddenly feeling sweaty and uncomfortable in her tartan blazer and pleated skirt.

"Wouldn't you like friends like that?" Emerald whispered in Felicia's ear.

"No!" Felicia answered a bit too quickly.

Emerald felt discouraged. "Well, maybe I should leave you alone to think things over for a while, Felicia. You see," she confessed, "right now, I can't think of another thing that I can do for you . . ."

"Am I a hopeless case or something?" Felicia asked sarcastically.

"Of course not," Emerald insisted.

Felicia's face softened, but she covered it up with a smirk. "See you," she said breezily.

As Felicia got up to go home, she saw another Post-it note, this time on a lamppost. WE KNOW WHO YOU ARE! IF YOU CONFESS NOW, YOU MIGHT NOT GO TO JAIL!

Felicia shivered. She glanced quickly at the members of the Angel Club across the street.

Toby noticed Felicia looking. *"Psst!"* She nudged Rachel. "Felicia is watching us from across the street."

"I know. I can hear her bracelets jingling." Val scowled. "She's probably planning her next vicious trick on us."

"You know"—Rachel's face grew wistful—

84

"maybe it isn't fair thinking the worst of Felicia all the time."

Toby glared at Rachel. "Do I have to remind you that Felicia once wrongly accused you of stealing my money? The very same Felicia who kidnapped a dog from your mom's kennel last fall?"

Rachel shrugged. "But people can change . . ."

Felicia turned toward home and started walking. She soon passed Sally Jillian, who was jogging with her dog, Romeo. Felicia remembered the day she sneaked into Rachel's mother's office and took the mayor's puppy, Hercules. Oh, he had felt so soft in her hand!

Felicia had wanted to keep the dog forever, to care for him, and make him healthy again. But she knew what her father would say: "Take it back where you got it! Dogs are scruffy and dirty." That's why she had abandoned the puppy in the woods. How relieved she had been when Rachel found him!

As Felicia trudged home, she couldn't help remembering Emerald's question. *When* was *the last time I felt happy?*

She couldn't come up with an answer.

9

At Home and in Heaven

Felicia thought about fun all the way home. At first, having to run after Emerald had made her mad, but by the time they'd stopped, she had been laughing even harder than her angel. She smiled, remembering that.

She walked through the back door of the McWithers' house with a smile still on her face. Her mother was at the stove, heating a kettle of water for tea.

"Hi, Mom!" called Felicia.

Felicia's mother took one look at her daughter and turned pale. "Whatever have you been doing? You look like something the cat dragged in! And you smell even worse."

"Um," said Felicia, her smile gone, "I was running around with a friend after school. I guess I got a little sweaty."

"Running around with a friend? That is hardly the sort of activity for which your father and I have raised you. A little sweaty? If you want exercise, you can join my gym and I'll get you some special workout clothing. Look what you have done to your blazer! Put it right in the dry-cleaning hamper and take a shower this minute. I won't have your father seeing you this way. He's had a difficult day, and I just know your behavior would upset him."

"Yes, Mother," said Felicia meekly. For some reason, her eyes began to prick with tears, and suddenly she felt very tired. Maybe she shouldn't have run after Emerald. It only meant trouble.

The shower felt good and Felicia replayed the afternoon in her head. Ms. Fisher had helped her with fractions, and then Emerald and she had played together. It had been fun.

Emerald had flown up to the Angel Academy after leaving Felicia. She had to admit that she herself was a little winded from her run. *Maybe a little nap in this little cloud will refresh me. And keep me out of Florinda's way* . . .

No sooner had she begun to doze than she felt a hand on her shoulder, shaking her none too gently.

"What in heaven's name are you doing here?" demanded Amber.

Emerald opened one eye.

"What's wrong? You look like *you* need a guardian angel!" said Amber a little more compassionately.

"Amber . . ." Emerald hesitated, opening both eyes. "I'm having trouble with my girl. Of course, it's partly my fault. Felicia really needs a more experienced angel. I don't think I am getting anywhere with her."

"To tell you the truth, Emerald," began Amber, flopping down next to the little angel, "I'm having trouble, too. Val's stepfather and mother are going to lose the newspaper if this mystery isn't solved."

Emerald began to blush, which was very noticeable under her green hair. Amber stared at her.

"Emerald! You are hiding something from me! That's why you blushed. You're supposed to be on *my* side!"

"Now, don't get all riled," Emerald said nervously.

"C'mon, tell me," Amber insisted. "Or would you rather we go talk to Florinda about it? I was on my way there, anyway."

"It's just that—have you noticed the little yellow paper signs that are appearing in Angel Corners?

Whoever wrote them says they know who rewrote Val's column."

"Yes, I've seen them. So?"

"Well, I saw Felicia reading one, and I thought I heard her say something."

"What?" asked Amber in exasperation.

"Something like, 'I wonder who knows about me?' " Emerald cringed as she said the words. She felt like she was snitching. "But I didn't hear her clearly, and she could have been saying something else. She swore to me that she didn't do it, Amber. And I trust her."

"Well, Felicia McWithers doesn't have the best reputation in town," Amber reminded Emerald.

"But she's not that bad, deep down," said Emerald. "She's just living in a big old house where her parents don't really care who she is. They just want her to be what *they* want, not what she wants."

"Nevertheless—"

"And what about Zeb Burgess?" asked Emerald. "He had plenty of opportunity to change Val's column. Besides, you and I know he's not as trustworthy as everyone thinks."

"Emerald!" Amber gasped. "That's privileged information. You are not to go around spreading rumors. The truth will come out in time. After all, the police know about Zeb and so does Val's dad."

"You see? It *isn't* clear who did it!" Emerald insisted. "Besides, isn't Florinda always saying that we can't alter things on earth? That we can only help our girls face their problems and discover their strengths?"

"You're right." Amber nodded. "And we really should be down there on earth, watching and waiting. It's just that sometimes it is so hard to know what to do!"

"You're telling me!" cried Emerald. "I just ran a hundred-yard dash, being chased by Felicia."

"Why, in heaven's name?" asked Amber.

"I don't even know, except that when I left, she was smiling."

"Well, that's something, I suppose." Amber understood Emerald's frustration. "But, listen. If you find out any more about whether Felicia really did sabotage Val's column, you'd better tell me right away. Remember, you're down there to help me!"

"Yes, ma'am," replied Emerald with a sneaky grin.

10

Whodunit?

Amber flew into the *Gazette* offices. She intended to visit the scene of the crime one more time. When she arrived, Val's father was talking to Mayor Witty on the phone.

"I know the whole town's reputation is ruined, and I'm doing my best to find the culprit!" Mr. McCall slammed down the phone, looking pale and worried.

A moment later, Sheriff Perkins came lumbering in. He was a big man, with shaggy white eyebrows. The strong scent of Old Spice always accompanied him.

"I just got some fingerprints back from the lab," the sheriff began. "I'm astonished at what I found.

Can you call Val and ask her to come down? I need to talk to her, and to Zeb Burgess, too. But don't tell Val I'm asking him to come."

Before Mr. McCall picked up the phone, Amber had flown away and reappeared in Val's room. "Your-dad-is-calling-you," she said breathlessly. "The-phone-will-ring-in-a-second. The-sheriff-wants-you-to-come-down-to-the-paper-right-now. He-doesn't-want-you-to-know-that-Zeb-will-be-there-too."

Then the phone rang. It was Val's stepfather asking her to come down to the newspaper office.

"Did they find the culprit?" Val asked Amber, after she'd hung up the phone.

"I think so." Amber answered.

"What a relief! We're finally going to solve this!" Val smiled. "What should I wear?"

The thought of Zeb made Val so nervous her hands began shaking. Each time she reached for a blouse to see if she wanted to wear it, it slipped out of her hand onto the floor.

"Before you ruin every silk blouse you own, I'd better help you," said Amber.

Val giggled nervously, but she stood still as Amber's steady hands adorned her in a powder-blue sweater and stirrup pants with a matching pair of blue sneakers.

"You look great. Let's go! I mean, you walk and

Val McCall, Ace Reporter?

I'll fly," Amber explained. "I don't dare fly you there. There's no fog today, and we might be seen."

Val passed another Post-it note on the way to the newspaper office. It read: THE CULPRIT WHO WROTE VAL'S COLUMN IS CLOSE TO ARREST!

Who is writing these notes? Val wondered.

A few minutes later, she was at the office.

"Val, we think we have a break in the case," said Sheriff Perkins. "I'd like to ask you a few questions."

"Okay." Val felt comfortable with Sheriff Perkins. She'd known him all her life. "Ask away," she said.

"Was Zeb Burgess at the *Gazette* last Friday, when this incident occurred?"

"Um . . . yes," Val nodded.

"As far as you know, can Zeb work a computer?"

Val thought for a moment. Then she said, "Yes. Zeb's always renting Nintendo games from Starlight Video, and he's got a CD-ROM, too."

"If you knew both of these facts—that Zeb was at the *Gazette* on Friday and that he can run a computer—why didn't you mention Zeb as a possible suspect, Val?"

"Zeb? A suspect?" Val asked innocently.

"Yes." The sheriff stared at her intently. "Zeb's fingerprints were found on your computer."

"No!" Val gasped.

"The fingerprints on your computer match the fingerprints we have on file for Zeb. One hundred percent," said the sheriff, shaking his head sadly.

"But, why do you have Zeb's fingerprints on file, Sheriff?" asked Val in a daze from this new development.

Val's father jumped into the conversation. "Val, this is confidential information, but Zeb was hired here as part of the First Offenders' Program. He was caught vandalizing a newspaper vending machine some months ago, and since his crime was minor and it was his first offense, Zeb was placed here to work off his punishment by delivering papers. You wrote about the program in one of your columns, remember?"

Val was speechless. *Zeb? A first offender? A vandal?*

"Remember what your father said about this being confidential, Val," said Sheriff Perkins. "Once Zeb has worked off his hours of service, his record will be wiped clean."

Val found her voice. "But, Zeb would never do anything like this. Besides, I asked him, and he said he didn't."

Sheriff Perkins and Mr. McCall gave each other a meaningful look over Val's head, a look that said they weren't so ready to believe a first offender.

"Zeb's on his way down here now," said the sheriff. "I'd like you to stay to answer any other questions that arise so we can piece together how all this happened—and why."

"I can't!" Val protested.

"Why not?" asked the sheriff.

"It's too awful!" A wave of panic swept over Val. "Don't make me! Please?" and before anyone could stop her, she grabbed her jacket and ran out the door.

Amber was waiting for her on the steps. She'd been in the office and had heard every word. "Are you all right, Val?"

"Oh, this is so horrible!" Val ran down the street. "Zeb Burgess, of all people. I don't believe it. I just don't."

"I'm shocked, too," admitted Amber. "I would never have expected it of Zeb, and I'm usually such a good judge of character."

Val stopped in the middle of the sidewalk. "Amber, I don't think there's anything you can do for me right now. I'm going over to Lulu's." She paused, seeing Amber's hurt expression. "I'm sorry, but she's my best friend, and I have to talk to her."

"Oh, no, dear," said Amber, "I understand. Call me later if you want to talk. I am here when you need me."

"You are an angel," Val said with a thin smile. Amber bent over and kissed her on the cheek.

"So are you," she said, and then she was gone.

When she flew off, Amber headed straight back to the newspaper office to see how things were going. *Val may not need me at the moment, but I'd better be prepared for the future.*

"No way it's Zeb!" Lulu gasped.

"But his fingerprints were on my computer!"

"Maybe Zeb has a good explanation. Val, why didn't you stay to hear it?"

"I couldn't face him," Val confessed. "I was in shock and . . . I was scared to confront him. I just can't believe it's true!"

"I know how you feel," Lulu said sympathetically. "I was scared to talk to my dad when I was suspicious about him dating Sally. And remember all the trouble that got me into?"

"I remember," Val said. It flashed into Val's mind that her best friend had, after all, been arrested for stalking Sally Jillian. If it weren't for the fact that Sally didn't press charges, Lulu would be a first offender, too! That made her think twice about Zeb's vandalism.

"Try to be braver than I was," Lulu said. "I have to reshelve a bunch of videos I mixed up yesterday. Mrs. McWithers rented *Jane Fonda's Workout Video* and I gave her *The Night of the Living Dead*. How about if I call you later?"

"Okay," said Val. "I think I need time alone to sort things out. My head is spinning!"

A half hour later, Val heard a knock on her bedroom door. "Open up. It's Dad."

Val took a deep breath and let him in.

Mr. McCall stalked in, still wearing his coat. "Why did you run away from Sheriff Perkins?" he asked sharply. "He needed your help! *I* needed your help."

"Dad, I'm sorry." Tears filled her eyes. "I was just so . . . so . . . upset."

"How do you think *I* feel?" yelled Mr. McCall. "How do you think your mother feels? We're upset, too, but that doesn't mean we can just run away from whatever upsets us."

"I know," Val said helplessly.

"Maybe your mother and I have pampered you too much, protected you from having to face things."

"It's not that." Val said. "It's something else . . ." She wanted to tell her stepfather about her crush on Zeb. But it wouldn't come out right, not now, and it wouldn't help things at all.

"I don't care what your reason is." Her stepfather's eyes held hers in a steady stare. "Now listen closely. I'm going to tell you what happened after you left: The sheriff confronted Zeb with the fingerprint match, and Zeb denied writing your column. Then the sheriff asked him what he *was* doing with your computer."

"What did he answer?" Val asked.

"He clammed up. He wouldn't say a word."

"Really?" Val was puzzled.

"And that's when Sheriff Perkins blew his top. He said that because he'd known Zeb all his life, he would give him exactly twenty-four hours to come up with a reasonable explanation, and if he didn't, given Zeb's current record, he would have to arrest him."

"Zeb? In jail?" Val couldn't imagine her Prince Charming in jail.

"Now listen, young lady," Mr. McCall said firmly. "I want you to go see Zeb tomorrow and talk to him. There's a missing piece of this puzzle and maybe you can get him to tell you what it is."

"I'll try," Val said shakily.

"No, that's not good enough." Mr. McCall glared at Val. "You must *promise* me you'll do it. Look me in the eye and say you will."

"Okay." Val nodded. "I promise."

"Good. I want to wrap this thing up as quickly as possible." He turned around and left the room.

"Amber! Help!" Val whispered.

"I'm here." Amber materialized. "Shall I come with you when you talk to Zeb tomorrow?"

"Yes. Oh, Amber! It'll be the hardest thing I've ever done in my life."

Val put on her nightgown and got into bed. There was no escaping. Tomorrow was D day—or rather—Z day!

11

A Definition of Fun

While Val was fretting about Zeb, Felicia was doing fractions. She almost enjoyed it, now that Ms. Fisher had explained how to do them. It was almost fun. *Hmm. Fun.*

After her math was done, Felicia went into her mother's room to say good night. Mrs. McWithers was at her dressing table, applying Ageless Skin Moisture Cream around her eyes. "Mom," Felicia began, "what do you do for fun?"

Mrs. McWithers looked up, surprised. Fanning her face, she replied, "I play bridge, and when I win I love it. That's what I call fun."

"What else is fun for you?" Felicia persisted.

Mrs. McWithers began touching up her manicure. "Don't bother me!" she said irritably. "The Home Shopping Network begins its sale in five minutes! Come to think of it, that's fun, too, of course—beating somebody else out of a bargain."

Felicia left the room. *I wouldn't call any of that fun,* she thought. She found her father in his library. He was sitting in his green leather chair talking to the Tokyo Stock Exchange. "Buy!" he shouted to one person, and "Sell!" to another. Felicia waved good night. There was no need to ask her dad what he called fun. The answer would be business, business, business.

Felicia wondered, *If what my parents are doing is fun, why don't they look happy? Is it because what they think is fun really isn't?*

She went back into her bedroom and began rearranging the bracelets, rings, and necklaces in her jewelry box. "I used to think this was fun," she said sadly, "but it isn't anymore."

Felicia felt awfully lonely.

"Shall I play you a song on my flute?" crooned a soft voice.

"Emerald, you're back." Felicia perked up.

"Now, that's the kind of friendly greeting I like!" Emerald flew to Felicia's bed. "What shall I play for you?"

"Do you know any old Beatles songs?" asked Felicia shyly. "My mom won't let me listen to them.

She says that they were trash when she was my age and they still are. But, I don't think so. Could you play 'Norwegian Wood'?"

"I can play the whole *Rubber Soul* album, if you like," responded Emerald. "I love the Beatles!"

Felicia drifted off to sleep to the sound of Emerald's flute. It was like listening to a lullaby. She felt warm and cared for, even loved, by her green-haired angel. She had never felt anything like it.

When Felicia woke up the next day, she felt like a different person. She kept humming the Beatles' tune as she dressed and walked to school. In class, when Ms. Fisher called on her, she walked up to the board and solved the hardest math problem.

"Good going!" Ms. Fisher said.

Now that *was fun.* Felicia decided.

"You don't say?" Emerald tooted a quick song of celebration on her flute. Felicia was the only one who heard it.

Felicia found herself paying more attention in class all day. She even noticed that Val and the other members of the Angel Club seemed very worried. They were busy passing notes back and forth and more than once she heard Zeb Burgess's name being whispered.

"Zeb's not in school," Felicia heard Sam

Eisenstein say in the hall. "He's ruined his perfect attendance record."

Why is everyone making such a big fuss over Zeb? Felicia thought. *I would never have the kind of stupid crush that Val has on him.*

Later, after school, Felicia was walking home, alone as usual. It was an amazingly clear, sunny day. Felicia could see Angel Falls from the center of town.

Her mood darkened though, when she saw another Post-it note on a parking meter. WE'RE VERY CLOSE TO THE CULPRIT! THERE'S VERY LITTLE TIME LEFT TO CONFESS! *Someone knows,* Felicia thought, *but if they do, why haven't they told the sheriff?*

In a moment, Andrea and Sylvie came by on their in-line skates. They slid by fast, holding hands.

They look like they're having fun. I wish I could try that, Felicia thought to herself.

"Your wish is my command!" Emerald sat on a nearby mailbox. "I can snap my fingers and provide you with a pretty nifty pair of skates."

"Oh, no, I can't," Felicia said quickly. "Remember all the trouble I got into yesterday? Besides, Dad says I'm such a klutz."

"That's not true," Emerald said, her eyes flashing. "Felicia, you don't know how much fun you're missing."

There was that word again: fun.

"All right!" Felicia said impetuously.

It took only a blink of an eye for Emerald to change Felicia's granny boots into the latest model of skates—emerald green skates.

"Cool!" Felicia said, but then her heart sank as she cautiously skated forward. "Wow! These are slippery. I'm going to fall! I just know it!"

Felicia moved along slowly, afraid to lose control of the skates. She felt so foolish as Andrea and Sylvie passed her by again. When they'd gone to the corner of the long block and came back in the other direction, Felicia took a deep breath. Then she said, "Um, Andrea . . . Sylvie, could you show me how to do this?"

Andrea looked astonished. Felicia had never asked for help in her life! She had always insisted that she knew everything.

"All right," Andrea answered. "I'll show you."

"Of course, I *know* how to do this," Felicia blurted, "but it's been months now, and I could use a . . . kind of brush-up. That's all. Stopping is so complicated."

"Oh, I'm sure you remember that," Sylvie said. "Just watch me, and you'll remember."

"Of course . . . I knew that," Felicia said, as soon as Sylvie showed her.

She skated a little way down the block, then put

on the brakes. They worked perfectly. She began to skate faster and faster, with a wide grin on her face.

"You're doing great!" Emerald cheered.

"I love it!" Felicia followed Andrea and Sylvie down the street, going just as fast as they were. Main Street's shops whizzed by. Felicia skated past the beauty shop—where her mother got her hair done every Thursday—and her dad's bank, too. She wondered if her parents had ever skated when they were her age. She couldn't imagine it.

Felicia skated past Toby and Rachel walking home together. They ignored her and waved to Andrea and Sylvie. Felicia felt a pang of loneliness. Everyone had a friend but her.

Suddenly a golden blur materialized in front of Felicia, leaping over her feet. "Hey!" she cried. She was so startled that she lost her balance and fell forward onto her hands and knees. In an instant, she was lying facedown on the sidewalk.

"Michael Jordan!" Toby shouted. "How did you get out again? My dopey brother must have left the gate open." She swooped down and scooped up her cat. Then she rushed over to Felicia. "Are you okay?" she asked. "Do you need help?"

"I'm fine," Felicia said quickly, struggling to roll over and sit up.

"Are you okay?" Sylvie and Andrea skated over to ask. "Can we help you up?"

"I'm fine, I think . . . but my knee sure hurts," Felicia confessed.

Felicia took a few deep breaths, and tried to get up. Even with all the girls' help, it was a lot harder than she'd imagined.

"Looks like you need help." Felicia and the girls looked up to see Zeb Burgess.

"I think I hurt my knee," Felicia said, tears appearing in her eyes.

"Here, put your arm around my waist and lean on me. I'll take you into Derek's bookstore. It's just a little way down the block. You can sit down there and figure out if anything is broken."

Zeb supported Felicia with his strong arms. He guided her through the bookstore's doors and deposited her on a soft chair that Derek had for customers who wanted to browse through his books.

"Thank you," Felicia said gratefully, after she was seated.

"I . . . uh . . . have to go somewhere," Zeb said, "but Derek can call a doctor or whatever."

Felicia nodded. "Thanks, Zeb. You were so nice to help me."

"Any time." Zeb smiled.

Derek came over after ringing up a customer's purchase. "What happened to you?"

"Trouble in Paradise! Trouble in Paradise!" chanted Derek's cockatoo from his perch.

"Don't mind Ezra. Those are the lyrics of a rock song he likes," Derek explained.

Felicia took a handkerchief from her pocket and wiped her face. Then she told Derek what had happened.

"Those skates are tricky," Derek commented.

"No, it's me," Felicia insisted. "Even though that cat ran over my feet, I shouldn't have fallen. I'm just too clumsy. That's what Dad says."

"I disagree," Derek said bluntly. "Everyone falls when they skate. It doesn't mean a thing."

"Not according to my parents."

"They're wrong!" retorted Derek angrily.

Felicia was astonished. This was the first time she'd ever heard someone say her parents were wrong about anything. No, she reminded herself, Emerald had said it, too.

"Let me have a look at that knee," Derek offered. "First aid is second nature to me. I was a paramedic for a while when I lived in L.A."

"Sure," said Felicia gingerly.

"It's not badly swollen, though you scraped it up pretty well. Now, I'm going to very gently bend your knee, and you let me know if it hurts. Ready?"

Felicia took a breath. "Ready."

With the gentlest touch she'd ever felt, Derek began to bend her knee.

"It only hurts a little," she said, relieved.

"Good!" Derek grinned. "It's just what I suspected. What you've got is a bad bruise, nothing worse. Believe me, if it were, you would have screamed bloody murder."

"Bloody murder!" echoed the cockatoo.

"Thank goodness!" Felicia broke into a smile that instantly disappeared. "My parents would have killed me if I had hurt myself."

"How about some hot chocolate?" Derek offered.

"Sure." Felicia settled back into the comfy chair. It felt nice being in this bookstore and talking to Derek. He was so easy to be with.

Derek poured two cups of hot chocolate. Then he pulled up another chair and sat down beside her. "Zeb was terrific to rescue you and bring you in here."

"Oh yes, he was . . ." Felicia remembered his strong arms, his deep eyes, and his curly black hair.

"Especially with everything Zeb has on his mind," Derek continued.

"Like what?" Felicia had always thought that all Zeb had on his mind was weight-lifting.

"I heard that Zeb's fingerprints were on Val's computer the day that terrible column was written."

"Zeb? Really?"

"I found it hard to believe, too," Derek said

firmly. "But if he can't explain it, he's going to be arrested."

Felicia turned pink. She put down her cup just as the phone rang.

"I've got to go," she said, getting up. Derek was already on his way to answer the phone.

"Psst! Here are your shoes," Emerald said. She waved her arm and Felicia's boots were back on her feet.

Felicia hurriedly limped out while Derek was still on the phone.

CHAPTER

12

Z Day

On the way home, Felicia passed another of the Post-it signs. It read, IF YOU CONFESS BEFORE THEY CATCH UP TO YOU, MAYBE YOU WON'T GO TO JAIL. Felicia thought about that one until she got home. She found her mother standing at the front door, furious. She didn't even notice that Felicia was limping.

"Where were you?" Mrs. McWithers yelled. "You were supposed to take your first singing lesson after school."

"I'm sorry," Felicia began. "I was with a friend— a few friends—"

"With whom?" asked her mother. "Your father and I have told you to be careful whom you choose for friends. Remember, it's always best to think the worst of people."

"Why?" Felicia suddenly demanded. "It hasn't made you or Daddy happy." There, she had said it, straight to her mother's face.

"Well—I . . . !" Mrs. McWithers's mouth fell open. "What *are* you talking about?" Without waiting for an answer, she continued. "I'll discuss this with you later. Right now, I have to give the cleaning woman instructions on how to polish the silver."

But Felicia wouldn't let her mother get away. "And you haven't a friend in the world—except those you can buy or bully! And who cares about your old silver? A silver coffeepot is not a friend!"

Felicia didn't wait for her mother's response. She raced up the stairs to her room, ignoring the pain in her knee.

"Wow! That was something!" Emerald gasped from her perch on the windowsill.

"It was, wasn't it?" Felicia sighed. Then her face grew serious. "I always thought my parents were so smart. Now I don't think so anymore."

Emerald flew over and put her arm around Felicia's shoulder. "You were incredibly brave today."

"Me? How?" Felicia blushed. It was so rare that she got any compliments.

"It took so much courage for you to ask Andrea

and Sylvie to teach you how to skate. I know how much pride you have."

"Yes," Felicia agreed. "But I wanted to skate so much. . . . And it was nice of Andrea to teach me . . . especially after how mean I've been to her."

Emerald nodded.

"And Toby offered to pick me up when I fell. Just last spring I tripped her in ballet class, and she sprained her ankle. She didn't have to be nice to me. And Zeb . . . and Derek . . ."

"The people in Angel Corners *are* very forgiving," Emerald said softly.

Felicia nodded. Then her lower lip trembled and she burst into tears. "They are!" she wailed.

Emerald drew her close and held her while she cried. Through her noisy sobs, Felicia gasped, "I . . . I didn't know people could be so nice."

"You never gave them a chance," Emerald said softly. "Kindness is the most wonderful gift one person can give another, Felicia. And I don't think you've experienced much kindness in this house."

Through her tears, Felicia said, "I thought my parents were trying to help me by criticizing me so much. They told me that was the only way I would learn."

"Kindness is the best teacher," Emerald whispered.

Felicia burst into a fresh stream of tears. And

when she was finished, she felt lighter, as if a burden had been lifted from her.

"Emerald," began Felicia, taking a deep breath, "I have something to tell you."

"Yes, Felicia, what is it?"

"Zeb is in big trouble because of me. I wrote Val's column, and the only way I can help him is to confess. Only I can't, because my parents will kill me. And he and Derek and the rest of the town will never forgive me. And Andrea and Sylvie and Toby and Rachel . . . no one will ever talk to me again."

"I thought maybe you had written it," said Emerald calmly.

"You did?" asked Felicia incredulously. "How can you be my guardian angel and think such a thing about me? You said you loved me!"

"Whoa, Felicia," said Emerald. "One thing at a time. Did you write the column?" Felicia nodded. "So, what is wrong with my thinking you did?" Felicia was silent. "I do love you! I always will. But you did write that column."

There was a long moment of silence.

"Now, Felicia, what are we going to do about it?" asked her angel.

At the same time, Val was wondering what *she* was going to do. She had promised that she would talk to Zeb that day, but Zeb hadn't been at school.

"Don't you know where he lives?" asked Amber slyly. "I could give you directions."

"Amber!" cried Val. "You're not being helpful!"

"Think about it, dear," said Amber. "If you don't talk to him, he's going to be in a lot of trouble."

"Please leave me alone, Amber. I have to think this through."

"Val, you've been doing a lot of thinking all on your own, but very little activity. Maybe it's time you listen to your stepfather, or to me, and *do* something." With that, Amber was gone.

For a moment, Val felt stricken. Had Amber abandoned her? Suddenly Val lifted her head defiantly. *I'll figure this out in my own time,* she told herself. She took off the special clothes she'd worn to confront Zeb at school and pulled on a set of sweats. She tied a blue bandanna around her hair and set about cleaning out her closets. Whenever Val was upset about things, she cleaned out her closets. Putting everything in order soothed her.

Val had sorted her clothes by color and was rearranging her third row of shoeboxes when she heard Amber behind her.

"Psst! Val!" she said. "I see Zeb! He's on the way to the sheriff's office and he looks as pale as a ghost. This is your last chance to talk to him."

"Now?" Val took a look at herself in the mirror.

"I can't. I'm all dusty and look what I'm wearing."

"There's no time to change. Come on," Amber urged.

"Oh no!" Val felt lightheaded, like she was a soda bottle that someone had shook up. But she knew she had to do it.

"I'll be with you the whole time," Amber promised. "Let's go."

Val hurried down the stairs and out the front door. She saw Zeb right away, walking by gloomily, his eyes on the ground.

Amber gave Val a push. "Just a few more steps, Val. You can do it. Keep going."

"Uh—Zeb!" Val blurted.

He looked up. He looked pale, and his black hair was uncombed. He automatically looked at the ground again. "I've . . . uh . . . got . . . to talk to you." Val said before her mind went blank.

Amber prompted her. "Ask Zeb if he saw anyone else at the *Gazette* last Friday. Ask him about his fingerprints."

Not exactly looking Zeb in the eye, but looking at his left earlobe, Val asked, "Did you see anyone in the office last Friday?" It wasn't precisely what she meant, but it was close enough.

"Umm . . . I don't remember," he answered. "There was just your father and . . . you."

"You *saw* me?" Val agonized for a split second

over how she had hid in the bathroom and then sat in Zeb's chair. "Anyone else? Think!" Val moved a step closer to Zeb, and her friendship bracelet jingled.

Zeb looked at it. A little light seemed to go on over his head. "That jingling reminds me of something I forgot. I saw Felicia on the front steps of the *Gazette* as I was leaving. You know, she always wears jingly bracelets."

"You saw Felicia McWithers? Why didn't you tell the sheriff?"

Zeb shrugged. "I guess I didn't think it was important. After all, she was outside, not in the office."

Even though Val liked him so much, she thought this was a very dumb reason not to have mentioned it.

"What else do you remember?" Val was looking straight into his eyes now.

"Umm . . . let me see. . . . Now I remember. Felicia was putting on a pair of white gloves. You know Felicia. She's always so dressed up."

"Psst, Val!" Amber whispered in her ear. "I think that's an important clue. Even Felicia wouldn't wear white gloves to visit the *Gazette* office."

Val thought for a moment of all the Columbo shows that Lulu had made her watch. "I know! Felicia wore gloves so she wouldn't get her fingerprints on my computer!"

"Bingo!" Amber cheered.

"Val McCall, you are so smart." Zeb gazed at her with admiration.

Val blushed, but recovered quickly. "I never thought you were guilty," she told Zeb, "but I have to ask you something."

"Shoot!" He smiled so sweetly, Val almost lost her nerve.

"Um, why were *your* fingerprints on my computer? And why wouldn't you explain it to the sheriff?"

Zeb blushed beet-red. Then he gazed down at the sidewalk, kicking an acorn with his running shoe. "Ummm . . . I was going to write you a note . . . kind of."

"A note? What kind of note?" Val asked.

Zeb kept his eyes on an ant climbing a blade of grass. "You see, Val, I . . . sort of . . . um . . . like you, but I didn't know how to say so."

Val's heart began pounding like a drum.

"So when I saw your computer, I decided to write a note. But then I just couldn't. I stopped after the first sentence and erased it. And then I left."

"Why didn't you tell that to Sheriff Perkins?"

"Heck! I would have died of embarrassment," Zeb protested.

Val cracked a smile. "You'd rather go to jail than be embarrassed?"

"Well, I wouldn't go that far."

"You almost did!" Val's heart was pounding so fast she felt giddy.

"But, you know?" Zeb's face broke into a smile. "Right now, Val, it's easy to talk to you . . . maybe because you're not so dressed up . . . and you're a little dusty."

Val giggled. Now the two of them couldn't take their eyes off each other.

"This is very romantic," Amber cooed softly in Val's ear. "But you guys have work to do, remember?"

Val reminded Zeb of his deadline. As they headed for the sheriff's office, they saw Lulu, Toby, and Rachel coming toward them.

"We were so worried about you," Lulu shouted to Val, "we decided to come over to your house."

"Wait'll I tell you what's happened!" Val began.

"Tell them on the way," Amber urged. "Zeb's time is almost up! Get over to the sheriff's."

13

A Crowded Bookstore

But they never made it to the sheriff's office. As they walked down Main Street, they saw Sylvie and Andrea coming toward them.

"Val," piped up Andrea, "we have something to confess."

"We wanted you to know that we were the ones putting up all the Post-it notes around town—" began Sylvie.

"Only," continued Andrea, "we don't really know who did it. We just thought we could scare whoever it was into making a confession."

"So, you're the ones," said Val. Then she pointed down the street. "It may have done some good, after all. Look who's coming."

There was Felicia hurrying down the sidewalk. It looked like she was deep in conversation with someone, but only Amber saw that Emerald was by her side.

"Let's confront her right now!" said Lulu, and they all began racing toward Felicia, with Zeb in the lead. At the sound of pounding feet, Felicia's head popped up. At first, all she realized was that Zeb was there—just the person she had to talk to.

Felicia shouted, "Zeb! I was coming to your house to tell you something. . . ." Then she stopped talking as the rest of the scene came into focus. Terrified at the sight of the whole Angel Club bearing down on her, she turned around and fled into the nearest shop—Derek's bookstore.

When everyone rushed inside, they found Felicia holding onto Derek for dear life. "Please protect me," she cried. "Oh please!"

"What's the matter?" Derek was asking. "What's happened?"

"*I'll* tell you!" began Val.

"No, I'm the one who has to." Felicia peered out from behind Derek. She faced Val and Zeb. "I'm the one who rewrote your column, Val. I was on my way to see Zeb and confess, and then to tell you . . . I'm . . . um . . . sorry . . ."

"I knew it was you!" Lulu jeered and took a step toward Felicia.

Val shouted, "How could you do something so terrible?"

Felicia burst into tears.

All were totally surprised—not by the confession, but at the sight of Felicia. Had they ever seen her cry before?

"It's okay," Emerald was whispering in Felicia's ear. "I'm here with you. And I'm so proud of you for being brave enough to confess."

Derek put his arm around Felicia. "I want everyone to calm down. Then I want to hear the whole story, from the beginning."

A green handkerchief appeared in Felicia's hand and she dabbed at her eyes. "Go on," Emerald encouraged her. "The worst is over."

"I'm confessing because it's the right thing to do. My umm . . . friend, Emerald, convinced me of that. And those notes all around town were scaring me, too. I was sure somebody else knew already . . ."

Andrea spoke up. "Sylvie and I wrote those notes. But we absolutely didn't know a thing. We just hoped maybe we'd scare the person into confessing."

Sylvie's face lit up as she said to Andrea, "We scared Felicia McWithers. Can you believe it?"

"I'm . . . um . . . scared a lot," Felicia confessed. "You see, every one of you in the Angel Club is good at something . . . but I'm . . . I'm not good at anything. Everyone likes you all—especially Val—and no one even tries to like me."

"So that's why you decided to ruin my dad's business and break up the Angel Club," said Val angrily.

"It was stupid," Felicia said. "I know that now and I wish I could undo it. It's easy to see why nobody likes me—" Felicia's voice got caught in a sob. "—but I've learned a lot in the last couple of days about kindness, friendship, and even fun. My parents always taught me to feel superior to everyone else and that made me feel mean and do mean things to prove them right. But now I know they are wrong. I'm no better than *anyone* else, and I've even been a lot worse." After that, Felicia buried her head in Derek's shoulder and just cried.

Amber stood next to Emerald. "Did you know all along that Felicia did this to Val?" Amber asked.

Emerald turned away. She wouldn't meet Amber's eyes.

Derek picked up the phone. "I'm going to call up Sheriff Perkins and Felicia's and Val's parents, and ask them to come over. Then you can tell them what you told us, Felicia. It should be easier to do it here than in Sheriff Perkins's office.

"It will," Felicia said gratefully. "Am I going to jail?" she whispered. Nobody had an answer.

Ten minutes later, the little store began to get very crowded.

"Felicia, what the devil is going on?" her father asked. He came in wearing his blue Italian suit and holding his briefcase. "I left an important meeting—" Mrs. McWithers in her silk suit told him to hush up.

Sheriff Perkins came in, and the store began to fill with the scent of Old Spice. The sheriff took off his hat and silently surveyed the scene.

Val's mother and stepfather came in, looking troubled. "What is it?" Mr. McCall asked.

Felicia began her confession again.

"How could you do this?" her father shouted. "Are you trying to embarrass me in front of the whole town?"

Derek spoke up. "Mr. McWithers, Felicia is in terrible trouble, so I would think you would concern yourself with her and not with your own image."

Felicia's father flushed red. "Of course I'm concerned for her." He put down his briefcase and walked over to stand by her side.

"And if I were you," Derek continued, "I'd also try to discover why Felicia is so angry that she would do such a thing. I can give you a clue, I think.

Felicia's been telling me that she can't do anything that seems to please you and your wife, that you always demand perfection from her."

"Of course we do. We have a reputation to maintain, you know," said Mrs. McWithers.

"Nobody can be perfect." Derek stared at Mrs. McWithers steadily. "Not even you."

Now Felicia's mother flushed. Both Mr. and Mrs. McWithers were at a total loss for words.

"So, how should we proceed?" asked Sheriff Perkins. "Should we put Felicia through a juvenile court trial?"

Felicia gasped, but felt Emerald's arm reach around her shoulders and hold her reassuringly.

"Or, can we, as concerned adults," the sheriff continued, "come up with a simpler solution?"

Val's father spoke up. "I think we can. Let's say that Felicia writes an apology to the whole town and that her father and mother also take responsibility. I'll print it all in a special edition of the *Gazette* and then, I think, nobody will sue anybody."

"I'll cover the cost of printing that issue," said Mr. McWithers. "And I hope there'll be no need for a trial."

"Right." Val's father nodded. "We won't press charges."

"That's a relief. Thank you," Mr. McWithers

said softly. "We'll go home and write the apology right away."

"And I won't go to jail," said Felicia, relieved.

"You will be punished, though," promised her father. "You are responsible for what you did."

"I know," Felicia replied.

"And your mother and I will discuss our . . . um . . . relationship . . . with you." He reached out and took Felicia's hand. She couldn't remember the last time he had held it. "Let's go home," he said quietly. And the three McWithers walked out the door together.

"Well, that's that!" Derek beamed. "And now we can go on with the Angel Corners Tourist Weekend."

"Hooray!" shouted the Angel Club.

"I'm so relieved!" Zeb took hold of Val's hand. And he didn't seem embarrassed about anyone noticing it.

But not everyone was satisfied.

"Emerald! I want to talk to you," said Amber angrily.

Emerald blanched and fled straight up to heaven!

CHAPTER

14

Angelic Forgiveness

"Help! Florinda, protect me," Emerald shrieked, hurling herself into the Queen of the Angels' arms.

Amber landed at Florinda's feet. "Do you know what Emerald did?" She glared.

"Of course I do," Florinda answered in her wise voice. "I know everything."

Amber looked puzzled. "Then how could you let Emerald keep Felicia's guilt a secret, from me and from Val?"

"Everything on earth happens for a reason," Florinda explained. "It was important for Val to confront her fears of Zeb, and to find out that her life isn't always going to be perfect. By facing all this, Val grew a little stronger."

"It seems like an awful roundabout way of doing things," Amber complained.

"Nothing on earth is simple," Florinda reminded her. "The complications there could make any angel feel humble."

Emerald peered out from behind Florinda's wing. "Amber, if I had told you about Felicia's guilt, she would never have had the chance to grow, either."

"What do you mean?" Amber asked.

"I had to stand by Felicia and let her know I loved her unconditionally. Once she felt she could trust me, she began feeling safe enough to trust others."

Amber nodded and calmed down. "I think I see what you mean. Because Val grew up in a trusting family, she accepted me immediately. But Felicia . . . well . . . she has a longer road to travel."

"That's right." Florinda nodded.

Amber flew over to Emerald. "I'm not angry anymore." She reached out and tousled Emerald's green hair.

"I'm so pleased." Emerald hugged Amber happily. Then she gushed. "Isn't the Angel Club wonderful? Maybe one day Felicia will become a member."

"I wouldn't go that far." Amber shook her head.

"Now," said Florinda in a very serious tone of voice, "it seems that a number of angelic rules were broken on this visit to earth. Emerald, did you receive permission to visit Felicia?"

"No, ma'am," murmured Emerald.

"And do you see all of the trouble you could have caused her if you had acted poorly? You are an untrained angel . . ."

"But, Florinda," began Emerald, "I *didn't* act badly! I helped Felicia and she needed my help! I couldn't let her face this alone."

"Humph," snorted Florinda. "Be that as it may, you had no business acting on your own. But," said Florinda with a forgiving smile, "I think we've had enough explanations. The flip side is that you and Amber did a wonderful job, and this is cause for celebration!"

Florinda clapped her hands, and a host of angels appeared. Touching wing to fluttering wing, they formed a large circle around Emerald and Amber. Serena, Celeste, Merrie, and Florinda formed an inner ring.

"A dance of congratulations!" called out Florinda, and all the angels went spinning this way and that in flashes and blurs of beautiful light and color.

"Praise Amber! . . . Praise Emerald!" they sang as

they danced. The two guests of honor held each other's hands. When the dance and song quieted down, Florinda clapped her hands again, and a lovely pair of new wings appeared for Amber. Celeste, Serena, and Merrie stepped forward to help their classmate into them. Florinda clapped again and from above floated down a shiny new halo that settled around Emerald's head.

"Amber," said Florinda, "here is your locket with a picture of Valentine McCall inside. And Emerald, although you were not sent, you have bonded to your girl and now she is yours. Here is your locket, with Felicia McWithers's picture inside. May you both always be a blessing to your girls."

The host of angels cheered until the heavens rang.

CHAPTER

15

Anything Is Possible

That Friday night, on the eve of the Angel Corners Tourist Weekend—which proved to be an immense success—the Angel Club met in Toby's attic for their first-anniversary party.

The attic, with its murals of *Swan Lake* ballerinas and its soft, comfy armchairs, was where they had had their very first meeting. Toby put up strings of pink lights for the party.

A table was arranged with tiny sandwiches and soda pop. In the center was an angel food cake from the Antonio's bakery in the shape of—what else?— an angel. "Happy Birthday, Angel Club!" was written on it in pink frosting.

The Angel Club had gotten dressed up in their

prettiest clothes and had invited Andrea and Sylvie, two very special guests.

Andrea and Sylvie gasped when they saw the room. They stared at the floor-to-ceiling murals, and Sylvie said it was like being part of a ballet.

"We'll be dancing soon," said Toby with a smile, "but we have a surprise first."

Rachel stood up. "When I first moved to Angel Corners, none of us had an angel." Sylvie and Andrea gave each other perplexed looks. "But, now, all four of us in the Angel Club do."

"Right," said Toby. "I didn't even believe in angels!"

"Well," continued Rachel, "now that all of us have them, we have decided that it is time to open the club up to more members."

"I know two girls I want to nominate," said Val. "Andrea and Sylvie."

"I second the motion," cried Lulu.

Andrea and Sylvie gasped. Toby then stood up and shushed the general commotion. She took out a piece of paper and read from it.

"Whereas Sylvie Sawyer and Andrea Nesbit both understand the spirit of friendship . . .

"And whereas the Angel Club is founded on the principles of friendship . . .

"The Angel Club is happy to initiate both nominees into the club with the understanding that we will do all that we can to ensure that they, too, receive the blessing of friendship . . . and their own guardian angels.

"Will the founding members of the Angel Club please step forward and sign this proclamation?"

One by one, Rachel Summers, Valentine McCall, Lulu Bliss, and Toby Antonio signed their names.

"Will the nominees please step forward and sign?"

Andrea and Sylvie stood up—their faces wide-eyed and beaming with happiness—and signed their names.

"Do you mean there are real angels in your club?" asked Sylvie.

"Wait and see!" said Val.

"And now for the music and dancing!" proclaimed Toby.

For the rest of the evening, there was music and dancing and eating and drinking, and each founding member of the Angel Club told her story of how she met her angel.

One by one, the girls called their angels to join them.

"Merrie," cried Rachel.

"Serena," called Toby.

"Celeste," shouted Lulu.

"Amber," called Val.

Val McCall, Ace Reporter?

Even though no one could see any but her own angel, and Sylvie and Andrea couldn't see any of them, a soft, warm glow filled the room, and all knew that the angels were there.

"When my angel comes . . ." said Sylvie.

"When my angel comes . . ." whispered Andrea.

All along Main Street, the shops were dark, all closed up and waiting for tomorrow's festivities. All but one, that is. A light shone out from the window of the Angel Corners Celestial Bookstore, and inside, Derek was fixing two cups of hot chocolate— one for himself and one for his guest.

"Derek," said Florinda, who was settled comfortably with her feet up on a footstool, "you were wonderful with Felicia, and especially with her father and mother! They really listened to you."

"The McWithers are quite a challenge, aren't they? But, sooner or later, they'll come around. I never give up on my humans," said Derek, handing the Queen of the Angels a mug.

"No, you are right," agreed Florinda. "One can never give up. Now, where is your book?"

"Right here," responded Derek. He opened the book and flipped a few pages. "Let's see." He ran his finger down the page. "Andrea and Sylvie are overdue for angels—and I understand that they've been initiated into the Angel Club tonight."

"Oh, how grand," cheered Florinda.

"And Val's little stepsister Tracy is about to have a crisis . . ."

The light stayed on for hours as Derek Weatherby and the Queen of the Angels discussed all the citizens of Angel Corners who needed angels. By the time they were done, the Angel Club party had ended and the girls were all in bed. In fact, almost all of Angel Corners was asleep, except for one girl who was wide awake.

"Emerald, are you there?" whispered Felicia.

"Of course I am!" Emerald sat down next to Felicia on her bed.

"I want to thank you for all you've done for me."

Emerald beamed. "Oh, I've only just begun, Felicia." She reached out and hugged her girl, who happily hugged her back.

"Guess what," Felicia said. "My parents admitted to me that they haven't been perfect parents!"

"All right!" cheered Emerald.

"From now on, I think anything is possible." Felicia grinned. "Who knows? Maybe, some day, I might even be invited to join the Angel Club!"

"That would be wonderful!" Emerald smiled.

And who knows? It could happen. Anything can happen on earth. All angels certainly know that!

Fran Manushkin is the author of more than thirty children's books. A native of Chicago, and formerly a teacher and children's book editor, she now lives in New York City with her cats, Niblet and Michael Jordan.